Praise for Melissa Schroeder's
A Little Harmless Obsession

"Quite simply put A Little Harmless Obsession is a delectable, sensual and poignant romance that is beautifully written and that delightfully draws the reader into the dramatic and richly detailed plot and the compelling emotions of the characters giving them a highly memorable story."

~ *Shannon, The Romance Studio*

"What a great story, thoroughly enjoyable, and inducing purchasing sessions, snatching up the author's backlist for more reading enjoyment."

~ *Bella, Fallen Angel Reviews*

"Wow, wow and wow! Melissa Schroeder is back with a bang!"

~ *Valerie, Love Romances and More*

"A Little Harmless Obsession is a hot, sexy, fast and fun read that I definitely enjoyed."

~ *Angela, Joyfully Reviewed*

"This book can be summed up in two words. Freaking hot!"

~ *Lillie, Novel Thoughts*

"A brilliantly fast paced, erotically intense story..."

~ *My Foolish Wisdom*

"Well written and fast paced this is a book that should be on everyone's to be read pile. Voted book of the week by readers!"

~ *Mistletoe, Whipped Cream Reviews*

"A Little Harmless Obsession deserves 5+ stars and is definitely a recommended read. Really! Go out and buy this book."

~ *Tyhada's Place*

Look for these titles by *Melissa Schroeder*

Now Available:

Grace Under Pressure
The Seduction of Widow McEwan
The Last Detail

Harmless
A Little Harmless Sex
A Little Harmless Pleasure
A Little Harmless Obsession
A Little Harmless Lie
A Little Harmless Addiction

Once Upon an Accident
The Accidental Countess
Lessons in Seduction
The Spy Who Loved Her

A Little Harmless Obsession

Melissa Schroeder

SAMHAIN PUBLISHING

Samhain Publishing, Ltd.
11821 Mason Montgomery Rd., 4B
Cincinnati, OH 45249
www.samhainpublishing.com

A Little Harmless Obsession
Copyright © 2011 by Melissa Schroeder
Print ISBN: 978-1-60928-204-2
Digital ISBN: 978-1-60504-056-1

Editing by Heidi Moore
Cover by Scott Carpenter

First Samhain Publishing, Ltd. electronic publication: September 2010
First Samhain Publishing, Ltd. print publication: August 2011

Dedication

To the Harmless fans. You have waited for Evan and May's story and I hope it lives up to your expectations. Please know that their story is as important to me as it is to you. Thank you for your support and your many emails promising me death and dismemberment if I did not finish it. You blood-thirsty crazies are near and dear to my heart.

Acknowledgements

No book is written without help from my friends. It has been a long road back to my roots and to the writing I love. I would not have made it without some support. Thanks to Shayla Black, Kris Cook, Nikki Duncan, Joy Harris and Brandy Walker. Each one of you helped me keep my spirits happy in different ways. A shout out to my best bud, Kally Jo Surbeck. Always nice to have a friend you know will make you happy when you talk and know all your favorite quotes from *Dodgeball* and *The Holy Grail*. Thank you to Samhain for believing in my Harmless books, and for being a top notch publisher run by one of the smartest chicks in the universe, Crissy Brashear. A special thank you goes out to Heidi Moore for taking me on...poor woman, you have no idea what you got yourself into.

And to my family. Les, Audrey and Eliza, you have helped me through a tough two years while I drifted about. Without your support, I would have never made it back to shore. You are always in my mind, close to my heart and all that is beautiful in my world. I love you.

Chapter One

A ripple of pleasure shimmered through May Aiona the moment Evan Chambers walked through the front door of Dupree's. Her breathing hitched, her pulse doubled and dammit, her whole body tingled. Even as she cursed her reaction, she knew it would do no good. It had been this way since the first time she had seen him years ago, and no matter how many times she told herself he wasn't the man for her, her body ignored her.

And for good reason. Evan was a man who turned heads—both men and women's. Over six feet tall, most of it leg, all of it muscled and gorgeous. He possessed amazing gray blue eyes that crinkled around the corners when he smiled—which he did a lot. He had one of those classically beautiful faces, but the slightly crooked nose kept him from being too pretty.

He offered her his customary friendly smile that held no seduction, but that didn't make him any less appealing. "How's it going tonight, May?"

Inwardly, she berated herself for the way her heart tripped at the sound of his southern accent slipping over her name. She loved the way it rippled over the vowels, drawing them out. It always made her nipples tighten against her bra. She busied herself with straightening the menus, hoping he didn't notice.

"Busy. Jason called in sick with the flu, so we're short a

person in the kitchen. Boss is in the back if you're looking for him." *Please leave before I make a fool of myself.*

He winked at her and her silly little heart skipped a beat. "You always know what a man needs."

He brushed past her and the scent of bayberry and the Hawaiian night lingered in the air around her. She used all of her control to keep herself from turning around and watching his fine ass walk back to see Chris Dupree.

"That boy is nothing but trouble," Cynthia said.

May glanced over at her best friend and the boss' fiancé.

She sighed and busied herself rearranging the menus again. "I know. He's a man-whore and way out of my league."

"That isn't what I meant. Yes, he is a man-whore, but I think he is very much in your league. What I meant was that Evan has too many problems to count."

She eyed Cynthia, knowing that something had gone on a few months ago between Evan and her. Evan had been not too happy when his best friend, Chris, had returned from a wedding all excited about a southern bell he'd met. But somewhere along the way, Evan and Cynthia had come to an understanding.

"Everyone has problems, Cyn."

Her friend shook her head. "No. I think these go beyond just normal problems."

Interest sparked through May. "Really?"

Cynthia looked over at May. Her blue eyes widened. "Oh, no you don't. You are not going to fix him."

May let one eyebrow rise in question.

Cynthia held up her hands as if to ward May off. "I don't know what the problems are. I just know that Evan had a horrible childhood."

May shrugged. "I figured that."

"Really? I thought he kept that hidden."

"He never has anyone visit him. I'd think most people would take advantage of a free place to stay in Hawaii...especially at Evan's house."

She hadn't seen the inside in person, but it had been featured in *The Honolulu Advertiser*. He'd taken a dilapidated, neglected house and turned it into a showplace. Even now it embarrassed her that she had driven by it a few times. But it was on her way home since they both lived in Hawaii Kai. So she drove ten minutes out of the way. It wasn't like she had been stalking him...really.

"Not everyone has a family like yours."

Cynthia's sad tone pulled May out of her thoughts. She hated seeing her friend blue, especially since she was usually the happiest person May knew.

"What? Not everyone has a house full of males who can't seem to pick up after themselves. Let's not go into what my grandfather does every time I bring a female friend home."

As May hoped, Cynthia's face split into a smile. "I didn't complain, did I?"

May sighed dramatically. "I still can't believe he pinched your ass."

Cynthia waved that away. "No problem, sistah."

May laughed at Cynthia's version of a Hawaiian accent. No matter how hard she tried, Cynthia would always sound like a southern belle.

"It's hard for me to understand family dynamics because mine are so warped."

Cynthia shook her head. "No, y'all are wonderful."

"Remind me of that next time Danny decides to try to flirt

11

with you."

"I like coming to your house. If Chris were ever to dump me, I know I would at least have my choice of dates." Cynthia sobered. "No, what I meant was that you know you have someone there backing you up...you never doubt that your family will be there for you."

May smiled. "It's hard to imagine not having them. We've always been close. Especially since my mother died."

And even now, twelve years later, the pain of her mother's sudden death at the hands of a drunk driver came rushing back. It had been so sudden, so overwhelming for a twelve-year-old. She pushed aside all those feelings, knowing that dwelling on them would not do her any good.

"Are you and the boss going out tonight?"

Cynthia shook her head. "No. I need to be at the bakery by four am."

May shuddered. "There is no way I could do that. You have to be sadistic to choose to be a baker."

"Since Chris has been complaining, I'm looking for some help. So if you know anyone, throw them my way."

"The boss complained and you're looking for help?"

Cynthia made a face. "That's what I'm letting him think. Truthfully, Cynthia's is getting too busy for me to handle. And I would like to expand, maybe start a delivery service for offices in the morning."

"Oh, good idea." She glanced at the clock. "It's already ten o'clock. When are you getting out of here?"

"I thought soon, but now that Evan's here, who knows."

May glanced back at the hallway that led to Chris's office. "You might want to interrupt them. He could be in there for an hour."

Cynthia shook her head. "No. Evan hasn't had much time with Chris, and I seriously think there is something going on with him."

When Cynthia didn't continue on, May decided not to pry. It wasn't her business, even if she wanted Evan. May had hoped she might be able to move their friendship into something more romantic, but three years later, she was still firmly in Evan's friend category. She knew his tastes, knew he was considered a Dom, but he toned it down when he was around her. Now show him a woman who weighed a hundred pounds and had fake boobs, Evan was all over that.

Again, she silently chastised herself and turned her attention to Cynthia who was studying her with a look of understanding.

"So have you decided on an Italian cream for your wedding cake or are you still trying to decide?"

Evan leaned back in his chair and studied Chris. There was a fine layer of tension in the way he held his shoulders. Evan knew something was wrong.

"What's going on?"

"Nothing. A little busy in the kitchen with Jason out."

"Yeah, May told me."

"She read me the riot act about getting some more help. She wants to fire Jason. He's skipped out several times. Simon also told me he's been bothering May when I'm gone."

Evan frowned. "She didn't say anything to me."

Chris cocked his head at the tone in Evan's voice. "Why would she?"

Yes, why would she? He knew she had been backing away from him over the last few months. Their friendship now felt more like they were...acquaintances. Her smiles did not hold the same level of warmth and she rarely had time to chat. It seemed like every time he stopped to talk to her, there was an invisible barrier that hadn't been there before.

Evan shook off his thoughts. "I asked her when I came in what was going on."

Chris snorted. "She didn't tell me, so I doubt she would've told you. Hell, I doubt she even told Cynthia."

"Right."

"She usually doesn't have an issue, but apparently Jason was none too happy she turned him down. He's been a little pushy in his pursuit. I don't know exactly what went on, but Simon said he's heard Jason has anger-management issues with women."

Rage whipped through Evan, his blood heating. "What the hell are you running here, Chris? You allow your employees to be sexually harassed?"

Chris looked a little too serious for Evan's liking as he studied him. He had a feeling Chris was trying not to laugh. "No. First, I can't claim sexual harassment, not legally in the workplace, because she's his superior."

Evan opened his mouth to argue but Chris held up his hand. "I understand it's harassment without the legal definition. I don't condone it at Dupree's. You know that."

"But you allow this bastard to hit on her?"

There was another pause. "No. Simon just told me tonight. May, damn her, never told me anything. You know what she's like."

Evan settled back in his chair and frowned. "Just because she runs that family of hers doesn't mean she can take care of herself."

Chris laughed. "Tell you what, bruddah. You go tell her that. Make sure I'm around when you do. I don't want to miss her ripping you a new asshole."

Now that he knew what was going on with May, Evan decided to move away from the dangerous subject of the Hawaiian flower and to the real reason Chris was stressed.

He studied his friend for a moment then said, "Tell me what's going on."

With a sigh, Chris leaned back in his chair. "It's Jocelyn. Mama is worried, and for some reason she expects me to fix my sister's behavior."

"Her behavior? She has never caused you one bit of worry."

He released another long sigh. "When I was in Georgia I stopped in on her. She's thin as a rail and jumpy. Now Mama said she gave up her job."

That astonished Evan. "I thought she loved that job."

"She did, but she just quit and the only explanation she will give Mama is that she was sick of it."

"That's not like Jocelyn."

Chris nodded. "I know. I might have to go back to the mainland, but I am trying my best to handle it from here. Cynthia isn't all that excited about leaving the bakery right now."

"You haven't told her what's going on?"

Chris shook his head. "She would shut down in a heartbeat to go with me, but I don't know if that is a good idea. Her business is so new..."

"Yeah, I can see that."

"But, if I do go, could you keep an eye on Dupree's?"

"No problem, bruddah. Although, I do believe Maylea thinks she can handle it herself."

"True, and she can, but I'm worried about leaving with the situation with Jason. She isn't being honest with me about it which worries me. I probably won't be leaving anytime soon."

Evan shrugged. "Either way."

"So, what are you up to? It's a Friday night and you're hanging around Dupree's?"

A feeling of uneasy embarrassment swept through Evan. "Not sure. Didn't feel like going to Rough 'n Ready."

Again, there was a beat of silence as his friend studied him. "You don't feel like going to the club?"

Evan couldn't really explain it. How could he when he couldn't understand it himself. The BDSM club he had built with Micah was now the premier hot spot on the Islands for those who practiced the life. As the silent partner, he had taken pride in the way Micah had managed the club and the huge upsurge in members.

"Just don't feel like it."

"Do you need to see a doctor?"

The amusement in Chris's voice irritated him. "What the hell is the problem? So I don't feel like going."

"How long has it been since you were there?"

"I was there last night, for your information."

"You were there to play?"

The disbelief in his Chris's voice was not lost on Evan. "What does it matter?"

"Ahhh, the first of the month, so you and Micah had your regular get-together over the books." His quick smile irritated Evan. "That doesn't count."

With an aggravated grunt, Evan stood and started pacing. "I don't know what to say. I just haven't felt like going the last few weeks."

"Really? I thought it was more like months."

Evan stared unseeingly at the pictures Chris had up in his office and did not answer.

"It's been since you joined Cynthia and me, isn't it?"

"Having a ménage with you and Cynthia has nothing to do with not going to Rough 'n Ready."

"Really?"

"What are you getting at, Chris?"

"From the time we met, you always had two sets of women in your world. There are the ones you look up to, women you think are too good for you. Then there are women... Well...Lee who used to work here. She's the type of woman you think you deserve. Cynthia doesn't fit into your idea of the kind of woman who would enjoy the lifestyle. You think that any good girl would never be interested in bondage and submission. You have a warped view of women."

Evan spun around. "And just what do you expect with my mother and the way I was raised? Jesus, the fact I'm not a serial killer is surprising if you ask me."

Sympathy stamped Chris's features. "I know. I'm not blaming you. I just think you need to figure out what you want. Apparently it isn't the normal sub you can pick up at Rough 'n Ready."

Evan rolled his shoulders. "I'm fine. Just been working on that new resort, putting in a lot of hours."

Chris wanted to say more. Evan could see it on his face. They'd been friends long enough to be able to read each other's expressions. Evan thanked God for giving Chris some tact, and at least some mercy.

"I gotta get going. Cynthia had a long day and she has a four o'clock call in the morning."

"You're leaving May here by herself?"

Chris rose to his feet. "She has a whole staff here. I do it all the time."

Evan frowned. "Maybe I'll hang around and make sure she doesn't have any problems."

"Just don't piss her off. She'll come to me about it and bruddah, you're my best friend, but I'm not protecting you from May."

Evan sneered. "You're afraid of a woman?"

"This just isn't a woman. This is Maylea, head of the Aiona family. She can kick your ass with just a few sentences." He opened the door and Evan followed him down the hall, the scents and sounds of Dupree's now more prevalent.

"If people at Rough 'n Ready could see you now." Evan snickered. "Done in by a woman."

"*Please.* I have always had respect for strong women, starting with my mother."

They stepped into the restaurant and Chris smiled. Evan followed his line of vision and saw Cynthia standing at the hostess stand talking to May. A sharp twist of envy clawed at Evan's heart. He would never begrudge his best friend the happiness he'd found with his magnolia, but there were times like today when he would give just about anything to have a woman like her. Their new relationship had set off a wave of yearning that Evan was just not ready to deal with. He knew it was impossible, but it didn't keep him from wanting it.

He shifted his attention to May, who was now talking to an older man. Dressed in a brand new tropical shirt along with the guidebook he carried, he screamed tourist. She pulled out two menus as she smiled at the man. She turned and said something over her shoulder. He couldn't hear the words, but the sense of her voice, the soft lyrical incantation, was one he knew well. As he watched them walk to the table, he ground his teeth together as he watched the man—who was old enough to be her father—slip his gaze down her body. *Dirty old bastard.*

"Did you say something?" Chris asked.

Evan glanced at him and found his friend staring at him as if he'd lost his mind.

"No." Evan inwardly winced at his curt tone, but he kept his features smooth.

Chris studied him for a second then said, "Hmm."

Cynthia walked up to them. "You ready?"

"Sure, honey." Evan smiled.

Chris shoved him aside and took Cynthia into his arms to give her a hard, smacking kiss. "Yeah, everything's done. Evan's going to play guard dog for me tonight."

She glanced over at him, her blue gaze studying him. "On a Friday night?"

"Why does everyone keep bringing that up? So it's Friday night."

She laughed. "No problem. Just Evan Chambers is usually busy on Friday nights."

He rolled his eyes. "It's been a long week."

Her eyes danced but she said nothing else.

"If you have any problems call my cell." Chris said. "I doubt that jackass will show up tonight since he called in sick, but just in case."

Evan nodded, but his attention was already back to May, who had the damned audacity to still be talking to the tourist. Just what the hell was she doing? She smiled at the man and laughed at something he said.

"Something wrong?"

Evan whipped his head around to see one of the busboys staring at him with trepidation. The young man glanced down and it was then Evan realized he had fisted his hands. He forced himself to relax.

"No, nothing wrong."

He decided he needed a drink and intercepted May on his way to the bar. "Don't you think he is a little old for you?"

Her brow furrowed. "What?"

"Grandpa." He motioned with his head over to the man she had just seated. "Don't you think he is a little old for you?"

She laughed. "I was just doing my job."

"Since when did Dupree's double as a brothel?"

For a moment, a look of confusion moved over her face before embarrassment and then anger took over. Her Caribbean blue eyes sparked with fury. "What the hell are you talking about? I was talking to him, which is part of my job."

The last was said as if she were talking to an idiot. Which, he wasn't too sure he wasn't.

"Is that the way you talked to Jason?"

The color that had flushed her face in anger now drained. "What?"

He regretted his comment immediately. "I'm sorry, but Simon had a talk with Chris."

She stomped her foot. "Boss and I are going to have a discussion tomorrow. Why did he tell you and not talk to me about it?"

"He had other things on his mind...wanted to avoid talking about them. And I guess the better question is why you didn't tell him about it?"

"As you said, he has had a lot on his mind. Lots of calls from the family, so I didn't want to bother him. And to answer your rude question, no, I did not speak to Jason like that."

"I'm sorry. I didn't mean anything by it."

She nodded and turned to leave him, but he caught her hand. He felt the slight tremor in her fingers when he touched her.

"I told Chris I would stay tonight."

She looked back over her shoulder at him. "Jason won't give me any problems. He called in sick, so he will avoid the restaurant at least for tonight."

"Doesn't matter, I'm staying."

She frowned. "Don't you have something better to do?"

He didn't know what to say to that. Because at the moment he couldn't think of anywhere else he wanted to be. Her skin was soft beneath his fingers. He used every ounce of his control not to pull her hand to his mouth and taste her flesh. His entire body heated and his mind blanked for a second more before he gained his composure.

"I told Chris I'd babysit you, and I'll do that until closing."

With a huff, she pulled her fingers out of his hand and muttered, "Babysitting."

He smiled as he headed to the bar and decided that at least he could do this one thing with a cool drink in his hand.

May sighed as she locked up the front of Dupree's. She couldn't believe how the time had gotten away from her. If her father hadn't called to check on her she wouldn't have realized that it was well past two in the morning.

As cool night air whipped through her hair, May started to regret telling Janice to take the deposit to the bank. It had been a good idea at the time, but May was having second thoughts. She wasn't normally this late, but Chris had enough on his plate and the schedule for the next two weeks needed to be done. As she glanced around the deserted parking lot, she promised herself not to do this again. She knew she was pretty safe, but she couldn't stop feeling as if someone was watching her.

Her beautiful little red convertible sat in a pool of light. She'd eaten yogurt for lunch for two months and had not allowed herself to buy any new shoes for longer to save up for the down payment. It had been worth it. She didn't splurge often, so it had been a huge thing for her. It was a sign of all her hard work, of how far she had made it. She was no longer the little girl waiting tables, but Chris's trusted manager. She had earned every penny to buy it and she was damned proud of it.

She rounded the hood of the car and gasped. Her heart was in her throat, her whole body freezing with fear. The door had been damaged, the mirror barely hanging on, and someone had taken a knife to the ruby red paint. Scratched into the paint, the word "bitch" was easy to see. She glanced around her, worried the person who'd done it was still there and still carrying the knife. May knew she had to get back into the restaurant and call the police.

She turned on her heel, her mind still whirling. Terror coursed through her blood and her heart galloped out of control. Visions of a knife-wielding maniac filled her head as she took a step and ran into a very hard male figure.

Chapter Two

Evan tightened his hold on May's forearms to keep her from running away. She thrashed about violently. The alarm he saw in her eyes and heard in her scream left him cold...almost frozen.

He shook her, trying to get her attention, to bring her back to reality. "May, it's Evan."

The pure terror he saw in her gaze pierced his heart. Holy hell, he didn't mean to scare her. He'd just thought he would make sure she didn't need him to follow her to the bank, which he knew was their custom at Dupree's. But she'd seemed not to hear him walk up to her.

Her breath was coming out in small little gasps, but he saw the moment she realized it was him...knew he wouldn't hurt her.

"I'm sorry," Evan said.

He realized she was shaking, as if it were thirty degrees out and not a balmy seventy-five. He took her hand and pulled her against him. "I'm sorry."

She shuddered. Every one of her luscious curves pressed against him. Without any hesitation, his cock twitched at the feel of her breasts touching his chest. It made him feel like scum, but he was only human. Needing some distance, he regretfully pulled her back from him and looked at her. Her face was still too pale, her eyes dilated in shock. She looked back over her shoulder at her car and he followed her line of vision. He saw the vicious word scrawled across the red paint and growled.

He shoved her behind him and scanned the area for the assailant. When he realized they were truly alone, he turned to face May again.

"What the hell is that?"

She shivered again. "Not sure. And I wouldn't have freaked out if you hadn't crept up on me."

He shook his head at her diversionary tactic.

He wrapped a hand around each of her arms and gave her a little shake. "Tell me."

Whatever he did must have snapped her out of her stupor and she frowned at him. "First, I think we need to go in Dupree's and call the police."

He wanted to argue, wanted to make sure that she told him just what was going on, but he knew she was right He walked beside her to the entrance and waited for her to unlock the door. The parking lot was deserted. Not even the sound of a mongoose or feral cat rummaging for food disturbed the night air. May locked the door behind her and headed for the office. Evan followed her back, but did not go in. Instead, he stayed within earshot by sitting in the booth closest to the office. He wanted to keep an eye on the door.

By the time she called the police to report it, called Chris and her father, he'd been waiting a good fifteen minutes. When she sat down opposite of him, he frowned. Dark circles smudged the delicate skin beneath her eyes. "You need more rest."

She started at the harshness of his voice, and how could he blame her? He sounded like a father, not a friend. Besides, it had nothing to do with the situation.

"I can take care of myself. I was up late last night with my brother, Danny. He's having some trouble in his entry-level algebra."

"I didn't know he started college already."

She nodded. "He's built for it, unlike Kai and me. He loves it." She made a face indicating her dislike of school.

"Now you want to tell me what is going on?"

She shook her head. "I would tell you if I knew."

"May."

"I'm telling you the truth. I have no idea. I know not everyone likes me, and I've made a few enemies when I've had to fire people, but most people I fire because they are lazy. If they are too lazy to come to work, I doubt the ones I've fired would have the energy to do this."

He mulled that over and silently agreed she might be right. "There has to be someone."

One perfectly sculpted eyebrow rose. "Are you saying only someone who knows me would scratch bitch into the car door."

"Well, why would someone who didn't know you do it? It *is* pretty personal."

She pursed her lips like he'd seen her do a thousand times before. It was a clear indication she was pissed. Too late he realized what he'd said.

"I don't mean that you are a bitch, just that—"

"If I had met someone they would think I was a bitch?"

"No." He shoved a hand through his hair. "That isn't what I meant at all."

She laughed, the lyrical sound bringing his head up.

"I was just fucking with you. I know my reputation, but I

doubt it had something to do with this."

He nodded. "Do you think Jason could have done this?"

"No."

"You just don't want to admit it might be someone you know."

"First, I thought of Jason right off the bat." The surprise he felt must have shown on his face because she nodded. "Yeah, imagine that, I thought about it. When I called Chris he mentioned it. But jackass Jason actually thinks he has a chance with me. He definitely wouldn't do this. Secondly, how would you feel if someone hated you so much they'd do that to your car?"

Evan couldn't answer because he had known people like that. Hell, he had been one of those people. Before he pulled himself out of the gutter, he would have slit someone's throat the moment they looked at him the wrong way. "No. I can understand that. But you will have to think about it."

She nodded. "I'm sure the police will make me evaluate everyone I fired in the last few years, but I doubt it will make much difference."

He opened his mouth to tell her he would stick around to help. Dealing with the police wasn't the easiest thing in the world, even when you were the victim. But the next moment, Chris came charging into the restaurant with Cynthia hard on his heels.

"May, are you all right?"

She stood up as her boss and his fiancé approached the table. "I'm fine. I told you that on the phone."

The last was said muffled against Chris's chest as he pulled her into his arms and gave her a hug. Evan knew it was just a brotherly hug, nothing sexual to it, but he could not stop the flash of anger that sparked through his veins at the image. He knew he had no right to even think of her as his, but the events of the evening had brought out his protective feelings.

Chris pulled May back and looked at her, then handed her off to Cynthia. He gave Evan an assessing look. "What were you doing here?"

Uneasy with the speculation in Chris's eyes, Evan shifted his weight in the chair.

"I told you I was going to hang around and wait. I would have left but I noticed May didn't come out with Janice and her husband."

Chris whipped around, faced May and crossed his arms over his chest. "You aren't supposed to be here with all the money alone."

"For your information, I wasn't. I sent it with Janice and Freddy. I figured it was a waste to have them follow me. I stayed behind to work the schedule since I'm off tomorrow."

"Don't do it again."

Cynthia stepped between Chris and May. "What Chris means is that he knows you can take care of yourself, and yes, the money was not here. But that doesn't mean anyone else would know."

Evan watched as the May worked out the implications and nodded. "I'm sorry, Chris."

"Don't worry about it. Police should be here any minute."

May frowned. "Over something this small?"

Chris nodded. "I called Janice and she got her husband to call in."

With a weary sigh, she nodded. "I need to have a little caffeine."

"I'll go with you," Cynthia offered, glancing at Evan then at

Chris as she walked by. He watched Cynthia slip her arm through May's as they walked side by side down the hall.

Once they were alone, Chris scrubbed his hand over his face. "Jesus, that took ten years off my life."

Evan nodded. "I scared the hell out of her."

Chris settled in a chair and motioned for Evan to sit. "Tell me."

Evan went through the evening, leaving out their confrontation over the tourist. Chris sat back and let out a relieved sigh. "I'm glad you were here. The guy was gone, but who knows. He could have been lurking around."

That thought brought a chill to Evan's blood. "I looked around, and I waited out here while she called you. I didn't see a soul."

Chris nodded. "While I appreciate you were here, you want to explain just why the hell you were this late?"

"Are you sure you're okay?"

May nodded. "I think everyone is blowing this out of proportion."

Cynthia frowned. "What did your father say?"

May rolled her eyes. "Nothing. When he knew that Evan was with me, he was okay with it."

"I would think he would want to come down here."

May shrugged and tried to squash down the little bit of her that agreed with Cynthia's comment. It somehow made her feel guilty. "He knows I can handle it."

"And just what was Evan doing here?"

"I thought he was gone. I said goodbye to him at closing." She frowned at Cynthia. "I'm sorry to get you out of bed. Chris shouldn't have dragged you down here."

Cynthia's face flushed. "We weren't exactly asleep."

May chuckled. "Then I'm really sorry."

Cynthia turned a brighter shade of red. "No, we were just...well, you know."

"No. I don't know."

The look of embarrassment on Cynthia's face had May laughing harder. Cynthia had a penchant for playing the Domme in the bedroom, so her blush tickled May.

"Never mind. I'll try not to be jealous."

Cynthia's eyes widened and she stepped closer to May. "You were attracted to Chris?"

May closed her eyes. "Oh, ick. That is almost like asking me if I had the hots for my brother. I need some bleach for my eyes to scrub that image from my memory." She opened her eyes and saw Cynthia's exasperated look. "No. Having a date...just the possibility of sex is better than I've had lately."

Cynthia nodded, knowing May's struggle with dating men. "It'll happen."

May shrugged. "Lately, between helping Danny with homework and my crazy schedule at work, I haven't had the time for a date, let alone get laid."

"Well, I see we stopped the trash talk that could be going on here," Chris said as he sauntered into the kitchen. It was May's turn to blush now. The idea that Chris had heard them talking was bad enough. When she noticed Evan standing there still as death she realized he'd heard the conversation.

"You shouldn't be eavesdropping," Cynthia said.

Chris wrapped his arms around Cynthia. "There are a couple of officers here to talk to you, May."

She nodded and turned to walk out.

"You want me to go with you?"

She could tell by the tone of his voice he wanted to, but allowed her to decide. Any other time, she might have, but for some reason she felt she needed to do this on her own.

"No. I'll call you out there if they have any questions."

She walked to Evan who was still standing there, seemingly frozen.

"Evan?"

He shook his head, apparently bringing himself out of the trance he'd been in. "What?"

She thought she heard Chris chuckle behind her. She was within inches of Evan. Everything in her body sighed with lust just being that close.

She licked her lips and was surprised when she saw his gaze drop to her mouth and follow the movement.

"Could you move?"

"Huh?" His focus was still on her lips. Heat brushed over her nerve endings.

"I can't get by you."

His gaze rose to hers and she thought she saw the stain of embarrassment on his cheeks, but she had to be wrong. Knowing Evan Chambers the way she did, there would be nothing that could embarrass him.

"Sorry. In fact, I gave my statement to the officers, and since Chris is here I'm going to head home."

Oddly deflated, she nodded and watched him walk away from her...practically running.

With a sigh, she followed his path but realized that he was already out of Dupree's by the time she sat down with the officers.

Evan bolted up out of bed, his body covered in sweat, his pulse beating like an out-of-control sledgehammer. An uneasy chill passed over his flesh, his body still shaking as he drew in big gulps of air. He looked around and realized he had just been dreaming—a nightmare he hadn't had in years—until recently. The sheets were crisp, clean, Egyptian cotton. The air was clean and pure. He wasn't in the dank motel room with his whore of a mother.

He scrubbed his hand over his face, trying to pull it together. It had been years since he'd had the nightmares, but they'd returned a few months ago. He couldn't fathom why, or how, except for the reason that his ménage with Cynthia and Chris seemed to be the catalyst. He was sure doctors would have a field day, but Evan didn't give a damn. He didn't want to get in touch with his feelings. He had banished the dreams once before, he'd do it again.

With an aggravated sigh, he slid out of bed and headed to the bathroom to splash water on his face.

He looked at himself in the mirror, wondering at the new lines around his eyes. He wasn't a vain man, but he did realize he was growing older. Maybe it all circled around to Chris and Cynthia again. Their engagement last Christmas had been expected. Chris wanted kids, wanted a whole brood like the one he grew up with. It was something his friend talked about all the time. While Cynthia had stepped out of her family's protective core, she still wanted the traditional family. Evan knew that wasn't for him—never would be. Not with his background, with his mother's tainted blood running through his veins.

Irritated with himself again, he grabbed a towel and wiped off his face. He turned the shower on and stepped into it without waiting for the warm water. He needed something to wake him up, pull him from the memories he'd just fought through.

As he lathered up his hair he let his mind drift back to Maylea and what had happened the night before. He'd definitely have a talk with Jason today. Chris wouldn't step over the line because the kid worked for him, but Evan didn't have that problem. Lately, anyone who even got close to her made him want to beat to them to a pulp. Now it seemed someone was pissed that she hadn't paid enough attention to them.

Granted, it could be someone she fired. Some people just didn't know when to let things go. In fact, the last person she fired was Lee. Even though Chris had wanted to press charges, her powerful father was a defense attorney. He made sure his little girl didn't go to jail. Normal people would have been upset, but Lee hadn't cared. She didn't like May, that was for sure, but Lee didn't like most people. She'd moved onto the next man, the next job, without batting an eye. She was poison, and he should have known before getting involved with her. Lee knew exactly what buttons to push with him, and he hadn't liked himself those few weeks they'd been together. But he'd been desperate...because of May.

The last few months had been hard on his control. May drove him crazy with those little smiles or the gentle, lyrical laugh that could be heard throughout the restaurant. Women like her attracted all types of men. She was pretty, but not truly stunning, not in her features. That came from within. Generosity and sensuality combined into a delicious delight that was hard for men to ignore...especially him. More than once he'd fantasized about her. It couldn't be helped. Even with the cooler than normal water temperature, his cock lengthened, hardened. Jesus, it didn't matter how many times he told himself it would be impossible, that women like May were not for the likes of him, he couldn't seem to shake the need that had coiled deep in his soul. Just the thought of her had his libido raging, his body ready to explode.

Needing some relief, he stroked his penis, closing his eyes and imagining that May was in the shower with him. That full ass of hers would be slick with suds as he'd slip his hands up over the rounded globes. He would lick the water dripping from her nipples.

She had full lips, and he imagined them gliding over his cock, pulling it into the warmth of her mouth. He continued to stroke as he thought of how her tongue would slip over the top of his balls, his cock, licking the precome from the hole.

His balls drew up and his whole body tensed as he felt his orgasm shimmering just out of reach. He increased the rhythm of his strokes, thinking of the way he would slip his fingers through her hair. The long tresses would tangle between his digits as he thrust his hips, shoving his cock against the back of her throat. He groaned her name as he came. He collapsed against the wall, resting his head against the cool tiles. Even in completion he had no satisfaction, no relief. It had been like this for weeks, and it didn't look to be improving. There was a reason he had spent his Friday night at Dupree's.

Evan pushed himself away from the wall and washed himself off. By the time he turned off the water and stepped out of the tub, he had himself under control. Almost.

He looked at his face in the mirror, wondering just what the hell he needed to push past this. He had done it once, knew he could do it again, but something told him this time would be harder.

Chapter Three

May pulled the long black dress off the rack and studied it.

"Oh," Cynthia said. "That would look fantastic on you."

May snorted. "Yeah, I'm sure my ass would look spectacular."

Cynthia didn't respond. May looked at her and wanted to cringe at the pity she saw in her friend's eyes.

"It isn't right for me."

Cynthia shook her head. "I think it is. You have the tiniest waist and this would make it look great."

It would, May knew that much. And she really wanted something sexy, something that would make her feel sensual. It had been so long time since she had. But if she wasn't comfortable, she wouldn't be able to even feel sexy.

"Just where would I wear it? I haven't had a real date in months." Cynthia opened her mouth but May shook her head. "I don't count those fix-ups my father keeps making. I rarely go out a second time with any of those losers."

Cynthia laughed. "Only you would call some of those guys losers. Wasn't the last one the owner of that new restaurant off of Pali Highway...the one with more money than God?"

May nodded but didn't say anything else. She knew there was something lacking in her, that she couldn't respond to those men, that she couldn't find something about them to turn her on. They were all basically good-looking, and Demetrius—the restaurant owner—had been gorgeous. But there was something there, something she couldn't put her finger on, that turned her off. They'd all been the most polite, gentlemanly, gorgeous men. There had to be something wrong with her.

She moved to put the dress back on the rack and Cynthia grabbed it out of her hand.

"What—"

Cynthia smiled. "I'm buying it for you, and someday I'll force you to wear it. Let's check out and go get some coffee and malasadas."

She opened her mouth to argue, but her friend just walked to the register and paid for the dress.

"You shouldn't have done that," May said as Cynthia handed her the dress.

She shrugged and smiled.

"And don't try that little innocent look on me, sistah. I'm not as gullible as the boss."

"Ha. Either way, it doesn't matter. I bought it, so you're stuck." With that, she slipped her arm through May's and dragged her toward the door. "Let's go get some of those malasadas."

Twenty minutes later, they were relaxing in the warm Hawaiian morning sun, watching people wander by on Kahili road.

"I'm going to have to learn how to get these fried right. When I make them, they are too heavy and greasy. Mine are not as good as these." She took another big piece and then switched her attention to May. "Tell me what's wrong with these men."

May shrugged. "They're wonderful. In fact, I'd say any other woman would be happy with them."

Cynthia took another bite and stared at her while she chewed. She said nothing, and soon May shifted her weight.

"Tell me."

With a sigh, May said, "They're just not right."

"In what way?"

"What do you mean?"

"Do they chew with their mouths open, wear too much cologne, compare you to their mother in bed?"

May shook her head. It was hard to explain to another person, especially when she didn't understand it herself. "So the sex sucks."

May laughed. "No. I mean...there's no sex."

"None, as in you have never had sex?"

"No, I've had sex, just not lately, and not with any of those men. Well, since Rick. Besides, I haven't had much success in that area."

"What do you mean?"

May paused and looked around. She wasn't a prude, had always thought she would be a woman with a healthy sex drive. But she didn't want anyone walking by to hear her discussing sex. In Honolulu, there was always a good chance someone who knew her would walk by and hear.

"I never really enjoyed sex."

Cynthia frowned. "I don't understand."

"I mean, I never..." Good Lord, she was blushing. She could feel her face heat. "Listen. You probably don't understand, but I just never felt connected with a guy to be able to do that."

Cynthia smiled. "You'd be surprised. Until Chris, there had only been two guys, and those were awful experiences."

"But not with Chris."

Cynthia shook her head. "No. He let me control things there for awhile. I didn't have control of anything in my life before Chris."

May knew there was something between them, something so deep it connected them in a way that no one could do anything to break them apart.

"So you practice bondage."

"You know that. But we're switches."

May nodded. She knew the terminology of the lifestyle. She'd been doing her best to learn about it for the past few months.

"But I don't think that's for you," Cynthia said.

"What do you mean?"

"Honey, the one thing all of those guys had in common were they were gentlemanly. They probably let you pick where you went and what you did."

May nodded again, knowing it would do no good to lie to Cynthia. "They were...boring."

Oh, God, she felt awful saying it, but at the same time she felt so relieved to share the secret with someone.

"Go on."

"They always waited for me to make a decision, where we would eat, what we would do. None of them seemed to be able make up their minds. I always seem to attract that kind of man."

"Makes sense. You have a strong personality."

May sighed. "I'm doomed."

Cynthia laughed. "No, but you might need to get a little more proactive about finding a man you can be attracted to. If not, your father will keep bringing home dates."

"Oh, God."

"Have you been reading up on BDSM?"

May nodded. "I read that one book you gave me, been chatting online with some people. I think I might know what my problem is."

"You're a submissive."

May looked around quickly to see if anyone had heard Cynthia. "Shhh, just what I need is someone calling my father and telling him I was talking about sex on the street with my best friend."

Cynthia laughed. "You make it sound like we're using a bullhorn. No one knows what we're talking about. You need to explore this side of you. You'll never be happy unless you at least try."

"Great idea. But I don't see any way to do that. I mean, I never attract that kind of guy. And I would not trust a stranger."

"You could join Rough 'n Ready."

She wished. "Too expensive." That was an understatement. The club was well known on the island as one of the most exclusive clubs, and it had the price tag to match the reputation.

"Maybe I can talk to Micah. He might cut the rate or something."

Hope speared through May, but it plummeted just as fast. "What the hell difference does it make? I would never be able to attract that kind of guy, then trust him enough for that."

"Listen, they have dedicated Doms there. It wouldn't be so much of a date but more like an experience."

"I wouldn't—"

"Yeah, you would. Listen to me. The men there are trained. They know just the kind of buttons to push. The worst thing will be if you don't respond and you find out that you aren't really a submissive. At least you can explore it safely. It isn't like you're going to fall in love with any of these guys...or anyone you would date, not right off the bat. At least this way you can see if it gets you going."

It sounded simple, so easy, but... "What if my father finds out?"

Cynthia snorted. "Then maybe he can find a man who will work."

"*Cynthia.* I really don't know if you can understand, but Oahu is like a small town. Yes, we have close to a million people on the island, but everyone knows everyone else. It could get back to him."

"Micah and his partner took care of that. There's a confidentiality clause in the contract."

"Once the word is out, it's out. A rumor is as good as a news broadcast here on the island..."

Cynthia shook her head. "If someone talks, he or she will get banned from the club...plus they have to pay a fine equal to one year's membership."

"Which I point out one more time, I can't afford. We're comfortable, but Danny's schooling isn't cheap."

Cynthia smiled. "I'll talk to Micah, and see what we can come up with."

Still, part of her hesitated. It was an excellent opportunity. Not many people get the chance to discover their inner self, find out just what they needed to feel complete. She had been fighting the feeling that she didn't fit in, that something was lacking in her because she couldn't respond to men. They were nice, they were attentive, and they let her take the lead in bed.

God...they were boring. Or at least, boring to her. Other women seemed to have no problem with them.

It wasn't like she'd never had an orgasm before. She had, plenty of times. Thanks to her battery-operated boyfriend and her erotic romances. It wasn't until one nasty breakup that she'd discovered her appreciation of the alpha male and his dominant nature in an erotic romance book. A man who would control her in bed, take the lead and give her pleasure. Reading one of them had been the first time she'd come, and it had embarrassed her. But...she couldn't deny it was the one thing that got her off. She had thought it was a fantasy, one that would stay that way. At least if she could figure out a way into Rough 'n Ready, she could figure out if it was the fantasy or the reality that got her off.

"Well?"

"Okay, call this Micah. Ask him if there is anything I can do to join at a lowered rate. I'm not going to be some kind of freaking sex slave though."

Cynthia offered her a mysterious smile. "I'm pretty sure nothing like that will be asked of you."

"What do you mean the police don't have anything?" Evan boomed.

Chris sighed, frustration fairly dripping from the sound. "They have no clues."

"The security cameras?"

Chris shook his head. "Not a thing. Someone tampered with them."

Evan's blood chilled at the announcement. "So someone planned this."

"Yeah, but I think we both knew that from the beginning."

Evan grunted but said nothing as his dark thoughts took over. The idea that someone had tampered with the cameras, then damaged her car...it made him want to destroy something.

"The worst thing about it is HPD thinks the guy sat around waiting for her."

"Waiting for her?"

Chris nodded. "Off over by the bushes there were a lot of cigarettes...a few footprints. I don't buy into it though."

"Why not?"

"Doesn't make sense. I mean, why stand around after carving up her car."

That car had been May's baby since she'd bought it three months earlier. He knew she'd saved the money, sacrificed, all to buy the convertible. Everyone in the restaurant knew it too.

"If the guy stuck around, there can be one of two scenarios. Either he planned on attacking her but I interrupted that idea."

"That makes no sense. Fucking with her car would alert her."

Evan nodded. He believed that was the case. "Still, having her scared would mean she's off-balance. That might give him the opportunity to approach her."

"The other option?"

"That the bastard got off on the watching her reaction." Just the thought of it had his blood boiling, his temper flaring. If Evan ever found out just who the fuck did this, he would beat the bastard senseless.

"You mean someone who isn't about attacking her, just likes the thrill of scaring her?"

"Hopefully, that's all it was. It could be worse."

Chris raised an eyebrow.

"Okay, what if the guy is bent on scaring her, gets off on it, but that isn't the only thing he is going for."

Chris's face lost all expression before his eyes turned cold. "You mean she could have a stalker."

"Yeah."

"Could be. But with one incident there's no telling. Could be someone she fired and this was just their way of getting back at her."

Aggravation inched down his spine and then circled in his gut. "How can you take this so lightly? There is a good chance May is being stalked, and she needs to be watched."

Chris studied him for a moment then said, "I think this is about something else."

"What the fuck are you talking about?"

"I'm talking about the fact that you want her, but you're afraid to go after her."

Evan shoved his hands into his pockets. "She's not the kind of girl for me."

"Please, bruddah, don't try and pull that on me. I know you too well. You wouldn't get so bent out of shape every time she has a date pick her up here if you weren't interested."

"Of course, I'm attracted to her. What man in his right mind wouldn't be?"

Chris raised his hand and laughed. "From the moment I interviewed her, she reminded me of my sisters."

Evan smirked. "I said in his right mind. You're not always in your right mind."

"Fuck off." He grinned when he said and there was no heat in his words.

Evan's smile faded as he started to turn the implications over in his mind. "I'm serious here about the stalker. You need to take this seriously. Maybe you can get her some hired help to be here in the evenings."

Chris gave him an odd look. "And just how the hell would I make May accept that."

"You order her."

Chris laughed. "Yeah, that won't happen. Besides, HPD is pretty sure she's not in any danger."

"They're useless."

"No, they're still going to talk to a few of our fired employees and an old boyfriend."

That caught Evan's attention. "Boyfriend?"

The idea that she had a boyfriend, someone she'd spent time with, allowed into her bed to touch her, to sink into her warmth and softness, irritated Evan. He knew he couldn't have her but he didn't like the idea someone else had. It was irrational and stupid, but he couldn't stop the jealousy coursing through his veins.

"Yeah. It was a few months ago. It was when you were handling that project on the Big Island."

Evan had landed a big job to renovate an older hotel and had been gone for most of a month.

"She had a boyfriend, dated him and dumped him before I returned. Couldn't have been that great of a relationship."

Chris shrugged. "They were dating before you left, but it got pretty serious. For some reason May dumped him. I have no idea why, but I do know that Cynthia said she hasn't seen anyone seriously since then. Anyway, since he was the last real boyfriend they want to talk to him. It wasn't the most amiable breakup."

That had Evan's blood turning cold again. "They fought?"

Christ shrugged again. His laid-back attitude was starting

43

to irritate the living hell out of Evan. He curled his fingers into his palms, trying to keep from wrapping them around his friend's neck.

"Well, did they or didn't they?"

He couldn't stop the irritation from seeping through his voice. Chris smiled, telling Evan he'd been purposively vague to get a rise out of him. Dammit, Evan didn't need this aggravation.

"Not sure. He did show up here once or twice bothering her. The third time, I banned him from the restaurant. He never returned."

"So, some guy shows up and threatens May and you ban him from the restaurant? What the hell took you three fucking appearances for you to ban him?"

"First of all, he didn't threaten her. He disrupted business, accused her of things, but he didn't threaten her. I would have called the HPD if he had. I didn't know about the first two. Just like the problem with Jason, she kept it from me. I banned him the first time I saw him, but she admitted later he had been here twice before. And for her to admit it, he had to have scared her."

Needing to move, Evan gained his feet and started pacing. "What did he do?"

"He said he wanted her back."

Something in Chris's tone had Evan looking at him. "What else?"

"Okay. But don't tell her I told you."

Evan made a motion with his hand but said nothing else.

"He accused her of cheating on him."

For a moment, he couldn't think. May cheat? Evan was flabbergasted. He didn't know another person who was more honest or trustworthy than Maylea Aiona. "Cheating?"

Chris shook his head. "I think it was more of the idea she was in love with someone else and he didn't like it. Not that May had ever acted on it, at least while being involved with him. But the bastard was convinced she wanted another man."

The idea she was in love with someone knocked Evan breathless. He was still trying to get used to the idea she'd been involved with another man...seriously, and now he had to deal with the idea she was in love with a man. Disbelief came first, followed quickly by irritation.

"Who?"

"I don't know."

"I thought she admitted it to you."

"No, what happened was he yelled it in front of a bunch of patrons. It disrupted business, so I banned him."

Oh, God, that would have mortified May. She might be sweet, but she was a tiger about her career, and she took her job very seriously. The bastard could not have known her very well, or did and used it to hurt her.

"How did he know?"

"He claimed someone told him. I have no idea who would have because I didn't know. No one had any idea here. Anyway, that's why the police want to talk to him."

Evan absorbed that information, then asked. "What's his name?"

Chris's eyes widened. "No."

"What?"

"I am *not* giving you the name of her boyfriend."

"Ex-boyfriend."

Chris rolled his eyes. "I'm still not telling you. Stay out of it."

"Fine." But Evan wasn't going to let it go. One way or another, he would find out who the bastard was and have a talk with him...man to man.

Chapter Four

Two hours later, Evan strode into the lobby of one of the most expensive apartment buildings on the island. The idea that May had been dating a celebrity and Evan hadn't known bothered him to no end. Why it mattered, other than the idea that he might be causing her trouble now, Evan didn't know. But it did. Just the fact that she'd dated someone seriously got under his skin. Whether it was Rick Simpson—newest weather guy for the local channel—or some other loser didn't matter.

He pressed the button for the elevator and tried to ignore the woman looking at him. He had seen her when he walked in, recognized that there was something familiar about her, but could not seem to place his finger on it. He glanced over at her again and she smiled.

"Mr. Chambers."

Her low, sultry voice sounded familiar, but he still couldn't place her. She laughed as he studied her.

"That's okay, boss."

All of the sudden it dawned on him that this was the head bartender at the club, Darlene...Darcy...he couldn't remember.

"People call me Dee. We never really talked before. I just served you a drink once or twice."

He nodded. "Sorry."

"No problem."

The door dinged open and they both waited for some people to exit before they both got on.

"Three please."

He nodded and pushed the button, then pushed the one to the penthouse.

"Ah, going up to see Simpson?"

That caught his attention. "You know him?"

She nodded and then made a face. "Not much. He's not my type."

He heard the invitation in her voice but did not feel the flicker of interest. She didn't play at the club, but there had been a few Doms interested in her, including his business partner. It should bug him, really worry him, that a woman who seemed his type didn't stir any interest.

"Do you know if he has been seeing anyone?"

She shook her head. "He was seeing a local a few months ago, but since then I haven't seen much of him."

Odd for a celebrity in Hawaii. Because of the size of Oahu, and the fact they lived in their own little world, local celebrities had a lot of perks in the islands. A weatherman on TV was well known and respected. He would have his pick of good looking women.

"You haven't heard of any problems with him?"

"With Rick Simpson?" She laughed. "No way. He projects the big bad alpha, but he's a pussycat."

The door dinged open. "If you have time, be sure to stop by apartment 304."

The tone, the look brought back a quick, hard memory. Micah and Dee had been having some problems at the bar...namely, they were fighting like cats and dogs. He knew

Micah well enough to know he wouldn't screw the help, but it didn't mean he wouldn't want to. His behavior with Dee might be a signal of his feelings, and while Evan had no problems with sleeping with staff, he didn't really want to fight Micah.

"I have a feeling Micah would have a problem with that."

She frowned. "Who gives a damn about Micah?"

He noticed she never called him boss...always used his first name.

"I think you do."

He hit the button and the door closed on Dee's surprised face. The interesting interlude had calmed his temper but not completely. There was no way in hell the bastard was going to escape him. The police had talked with Simpson earlier, but Evan knew they had to be careful with a local celebrity. He did not.

The door opened and he walked into the hall. There was only one door, Simpson's. Being a weatherman paid well.

He leaned on the doorbell.

"Hold on."

The jackass sounded irritated, but then he might still be pissed the police had showed up earlier. The door opened. A good-looking, bleach blond stared at him. His teeth were so white they probably glowed in the dark. He was dressed in an old T-shirt and jeans.

"Who the hell are you?"

"Evan Chambers."

Something that looked like a strange mixture of disgust and fear slid over the man's face. "What the fuck do you want?"

"I want to know where you were last night."

"I told the police, I was at a fundraiser most of the night."

"Yeah, they told me that. But what I want to know is who you went home with?"

Simpson's face turned red. "What?"

"The fundraiser was over at ten. That gave you plenty of time to get over to Dupree's."

"I came home. The police have no problems with it."

He leaned closer. "I don't buy it."

"Fuck you. I don't have to put up with this, considering who you are."

He moved to shut the door, but Evan slammed his palm against it. "What the fuck does that mean?"

"None of your goddamn business."

"Answer me, or I will make sure you do. I don't have to be nice to you like the HPD."

Simpson's face flushed with anger. "Fine, you bastard. I've been waiting for this for months. I wasted all my time getting that fucking prude in bed and what did I get? Nothing. She was the worst lay I've ever had."

Fury crowded Evan's vision, and like years ago when living on the streets, he didn't think, he acted on instinct. He grabbed the collar of the jackass's T-shirt and pulled him closer. It only took one hit to his nose for Simpson to crumple into a heap at Evan's feet. Disgust filled him as he looked at the bastard. Blood dripped from his nose as he shook his head.

"You might want to think of that if you ever want to say anything nasty about Maylea."

Evan was still pissed when he walked into Dupree's mid-afternoon. The lull between lunch and dinner had hit and he knew it was about the only time he could get May cornered. He saw her sitting at a back table rolling silverware up in napkins.

50

He paid no attention to the woman working the hostess stand and headed for May's table. She sat there as if she didn't have a care in the world, as if she had not been threatened and might have a stalker.

He could feel his temper start to boil, so he ordered himself to calm down. It wasn't as if the police were worried about it. They'd blown him off when he showed up wanting to talk to the officer in charge. There was a real chance it was just a disgruntled employee...except for the fact that she was watched. To him, that added a whole other level to his worry. Someone had wanted to scare her and get some kind of sick thrill by witnessing her fear. By the time he reached the table, his temper was back up again.

She looked up at him, a welcoming smile on her face which made his temper spark and flare.

"What the fuck did you ever see in Simpson?"

A layer of deathly quiet filled the air around them as he watched her smile dissolve. The clatter of plates seemed to diminish as everyone turned to look at them.

"I don't think it's any of your business." She pronounced each word very specifically as she tightened her fingers around a light blue napkin.

He looked up at her face, then around at the people watching them. With an irritated sigh, he pulled out a chair and sat.

"And I did not invite you to sit down."

He said nothing as he watched her pick up silverware and place it on the folded napkin. Watching her do the simple work seemed to calm him, bring him back to reality.

"Sorry."

"Yes, you are."

He watched her actions, her very precise movements and realized he had not only pissed her off, but embarrassed her. May believed in professionalism, thrived on it and expected no less than the same from her workers. "Dammit, I apologize. I lost my temper."

She looked up at him, one eyebrow raised. "What set you off?"

He was pissed she wasn't taking any of this seriously, but secondly, and much worse, he was jealous. He knew now that Simpson had had sex with May. The idea that she let that slime ball touch her was almost too much to bear. Even now his fingers itched to return and beat the living hell out of the bastard.

"I'm worried about you."

"Hmmm." She started her work again. "And just why did you bring up Rick?"

"He pissed me off."

Her head shot up and her face paled. "You've met him."

Her reaction was not what he'd been expecting. The wariness in her gaze confused him.

"Today. I went to his apartment to find out just where the hell he was last night."

"Did he say anything to you?" Her voice had grown tight, but again, he did not hear anger.

"He said some not-so-nice things."

He watched as her fingers tightened around the napkin of silverware she had just rolled.

"And what did you do?"

He studied her for a second, his stomach churning at the idea she was worried about Simpson. "I punched him."

She grimaced. "I wish you hadn't."

The idea that she cared he might have hurt her former lover fueled his temper. "I couldn't let him say those things and get away with it."

"He could have you arrested for assault. In fact, I would almost bet he would love to do that."

Evan shook his head. "There is no way he would do that. He'd have to admit that he was under suspicion for fucking up your car. It would be a PR nightmare for the station."

He realized his mistake the moment she eyed him. "So you went over to his apartment, antagonized him until he said something to irritate you."

"I didn't antagonize him—"

She held up her hand to stop him. "Evan, I know you better than that. You were pissed off for God knows what reason and decided to take it out on him. What did he say?"

He couldn't tell her, didn't even want to remember the vile words the jackass had said.

"Why don't you tell me why you are so sure that it isn't Simpson?"

She blinked. "The police said he was a fundraiser last night, all night. There's no way he could have made it over here."

But there was a way. It was only a fifteen minute walk from where he had been.

"It wasn't him."

He focused on her face again. "Why?"

She sighed. "Rick wouldn't do it. He...let's just say I figured never to see him again."

"Except every night on TV." She said nothing to that. "Why didn't you tell me you were dating a celebrity?"

She made a face. "He's not a real celebrity."

He shrugged. "Enough of one."

She went back to her task. "It isn't like I tell you about every man I date. You were working on the Big Island when I dated him. It ended badly, as most relationships do."

The defeat he heard in her voice aggravated him even more. "Relationships end."

She glanced up at him with wide eyes and he could not blame her. His voice had snapped out the comment in anger.

"Yes, but most people have hopes of finding something permanent."

Dammit, he hated when she said it. It irritated because he knew that was what she wanted. He hated the confirmation that she wanted something he could never give her.

"I want you to promise me something," she said, her gaze back on her task.

"What?"

"I don't need you bothering my old boyfriends."

"You have more men who have threatened you? Jesus, May, I had no idea you dated that much."

Now came the anger. Her face flushed and her eyes narrowed. When she stood, her body vibrated with fury. "I date. It isn't like I bring them around to you for approval. I'm not a virgin, nor am I a slut. But dammit, I have a personal life. And amazingly, there are men who actually want to date me."

He opened his mouth to tell her that didn't surprise him at all, but she rolled right on.

"Stay out of it, Evan. I don't need your help."

She turned on her heel and marched back to the office. Even being the subject of her irritation, he leaned over to enjoy the view of her generous ass sway.

"You can't leave that one alone."

He turned around and found Lee Apple looking at him with a mocking smile. Evan cursed the three weeks he'd lost his mind and taken the witch to bed. She was the antithesis of May in every way, from her slim, athletic body, the fake nails and over-done face, to an evil core.

"I'm amazed Chris lets you come in here," he said.

She rolled her eyes. "He tried to ban me, but then Daddy is a bit too powerful for that."

Lee had worked at Dupree's during their brief stint, and been fired. May had proof of her stealing money from the till, but Lee's father was a very powerful defense attorney in Honolulu. Needless to say, her daddy had made sure she'd spent no time in jail.

"Well, I would say it's been fun, but that would be a lie." He started to move past her, but she grabbed his forearm, her sculptured nails biting into his skin. "She isn't the girl for you and you know it. She couldn't give you what you want...she's too clean."

He shook free of her, his stomach turning at the memories of their time together.

"You could never just let things go."

Her eyes narrowed. "You never understood that being with me was the best you would ever have."

He laughed, but there was not an ounce of humor in it. "If you're the best, I'd truly hate to see the worst."

Before she could respond, he turned away, trying to bleach his mind of the images that bled into his head as he moved in the direction of his truck. It had been a bad time for him, one that he would like to forget. Cynthia and Chris had gotten together and Evan had been at a loss.

Cynthia had thrown him for a loop. She had pretty

manners and that soft southern voice, a woman who was as kind as she was beautiful. The idea that she was a switch boggled his mind. It went against everything he knew about women. Chris had told him he was wrong, and Cynthia had been his proof. And as if to prove her and Chris wrong, he'd picked up the vilest creature on the face of the planet.

He laid his head back and closed his eyes. Jesus, it had been horrible. Lee knew just what buttons to push, how to bring out the animal he caged. She liked pain. She got off on it, thrived on pushing her Doms to the edge to make them cause pain. Evan had been a little too raw when he'd hooked up with her, and the three weeks they'd been together had been some of the worst in his life since his junkie mother had overdosed.

With a sigh, he opened his eyes and saw Lee leading Jason to her car. Odd, he would have never thought Lee would go for a guy who could be led around...but who knew with her. She was one crazy woman. Evan just thanked God he wasn't tangled up with her anymore.

He jumped when someone knocked on his window. He turned and found Cynthia smiling at him. He rolled it down.

"You going in?" she asked.

"Nope, I was just in there and did my damage for the day. Did you know about that?" he asked, nodding in the direction of Lee.

She looked then said something under her breath. "Chris will have a fit if he finds out she was here."

"I thought he had her barred."

Cynthia rolled her eyes. "He did. Filed the report with Honolulu PD, went through all the motions. Hell, she pleaded out to the stealing charge. You know her father. He made some threats and when that didn't work, he went to the police. He still has some ties there and had her record expunged. But she hasn't been around for months that I know of. Wonder why she showed up today? I had no idea she was dating him or why. I would have never pegged him for her type."

"Who knows with her?" He finally took stock of the way Cynthia was dressed. The old faded jeans hugged her hips, and the short T-shirt showed off her new belly ring. "Magnolia, how about I tempt you into a little play for the afternoon at Rough 'n Ready?"

She laughed. "Chris would not be happy about that. What did you mean you did your damage?"

"May. I had a talk with that Simpson she dated."

She inched her sunglasses down on her nose and stared at him over the edge. "And just why did you do that?"

"Just asked him a few questions, but apparently May isn't happy I interfered."

She laughed. "I bet not. Just remember, May isn't stupid. If the police really thought there was a threat, she would take it seriously."

He still couldn't shake the idea that this was more, much more than anyone thought it was. "Well, since you turned me down, I guess I should get back to work."

She leaned in, the scent of cinnamon filling the cab of his pickup. "Try to behave."

"Where is the fun in that?" he asked, and she laughed like he knew she would. He smiled at her as he drove away.

His mind went back to Simpson, his accusations...there was something there that truly upset May. The idea she was still in love with the bastard irritated Evan more than he thought possible. It wasn't as if he expected her not to have a love life, but he hadn't wanted to hear about it. He didn't even want to contemplate her having sex with anyone...well, except him.

Immediately, the vision of her strapped to his bed came violently to his mind. He tried to push it aside, but for the past few weeks, he had yet to dislodge it since he'd dreamed it. She would look perfect there, her golden skin against the light blue sheets. He could almost hear her moan his name. His cock went hard as he imagined slipping up her body, licking, tasting, teasing her before he thrust into her, the tight clasp of her pussy surrounding him.

Someone beeped a horn, pulling him out of his fantasy. He had been sitting at a green light thinking about May...again. He scrubbed his hand over his face as he took the ramp to H-1.

Jesus, he was a mess. He had to get past this before he died from lack of oxygen to his brain. Jacking off every morning after he dreamed of her was just not doing the job. He needed a woman, needed one now. But whenever he even thought about it, May's face came to his mind. The other women left him cold, uninterested in the games he'd taken pleasure from for so many years.

Something had to give...and soon, or he wasn't sure what he would do.

Chapter Five

"So, I talked to Micah." Cynthia said.

May almost dropped the stack of dishes she was carrying as she glanced around to see who could be listening.

"*Cynthia.*"

Her friend's blue eyes widened innocently. "What?"

Steadier, May carried the stack of dishes into the kitchen. It had grown even quieter since Evan left. There weren't that many people, but they were still around.

"I don't want people to hear."

Cynthia shrugged as if it was no big deal. "Not like anyone will know what I'm talking about, but why not take a quick break outside. It is gorgeous."

May rolled her eyes. "We live in Hawaii. It's gorgeous every day."

But she relented, grabbing a cup of Kona on her way out the door.

She glanced at Cynthia, who was fairly brimming with excitement. "Well?"

Cynthia smiled at her. "Micah said he would allow you to pay only the application fee and you could get one whole year free."

That gave May pause. "What gives?"

Cynthia widened her eyes innocently. "What do you mean?"

"Micah wouldn't agree to it without something in return."

Her friend shrugged. "You just have to submit."

"Well, isn't that the plan? I mean, why else would I want to join?" May blew on her coffee before taking a sip.

"There are conditions though. It has to be public and it has to be with an owner of the club."

May choked on her coffee. "What?"

Cynthia waved it away. "It's really no big deal. I mean, people definitely go for it."

"But...you said publicly. I'm not really sure I can do that. And besides, it seems to be a bit too much."

Still, she couldn't stop the sharp tug of excitement at the idea. There was part of her that was appalled, but deep down, the concept of being in front of people naked...it was sort of a turn on. She'd had dreams about it for years, and more than once she had fantasized about stealing away for sex on the beach. This would be like trying out two of her secret desires at once.

"A single membership costs five thousand a year. I think it is actually not that big for what you are getting," Cynthia remarked.

May sighed. Even with her fantasies, she didn't know if she could do it. There would be no club for her then. She could never afford a membership.

"Well, that's that."

Cynthia grabbed her arm to stop her. "No, it's not. I want you to think this through."

Appalled, she stared at her friend. "There is no thinking needed. I can't do a public submission. Seriously, there is just no way. It is out of the question."

"Think. Micah is a good Dom. He is someone you can trust, someone who won't hurt you. And you know that everything would be handled carefully. You can't guarantee that with someone you get involved with."

That was true. She had read all kinds of warnings online about being careful. In the world of BDSM, there were some people who used their knowledge to control beyond the bedroom. "Still..."

Cynthia crossed her arms beneath her breasts and stared at May. "I was extremely lucky to find Chris. While I don't think there is anything wrong with the lifestyle, just like any group, they are going to have their predators. And they could use this against you in some way. At least this way, you're safe."

That was definitely true. "But in public?"

"Micah said he wanted to be sure you were serious about it. A lot of people would work a deal out like this and then just show up to troll for dates. Plus, he doesn't want people to come out of the woodwork asking for a free membership. If word got out, you can believe he would have more than one person trying." Cynthia smiled at her again. "You have a problem with that? I have to say, I might be a little nervous about it, but...remember that story you told me?"

"What story?" As soon as she asked, May remembered how one night over drinks she'd confessed her interest in exhibitionism. Her face flushed. "This is a little bit more than making out in public."

"First, your fantasy wasn't about just making out. Granted, this is a little more than going somewhere secluded to have sex." Cynthia shrugged. "If it's too much, you can call a stop to it. You know the owner of the club would listen if you invoked the safe word. And think about all the people you could meet there. At least there they have gone through the application

61

process."

That was true. But there was one glaring problem. The man she pined over, the one she had cried over and who treated her like a sister, might be there.

"What is holding you back, sistah?" Cynthia was perceptive.

May heaved a sigh. "Evan."

Cynthia nodded. "He doesn't really come around that much anymore. I mean, he hangs out with Chris and Micah but it's been several months since he's been there looking for a sub."

May's heart sank a little and she silently chastised herself for it. He wasn't her concern anymore. Just because he wasn't going to the club anymore, and that probably meant he had someone fulfilling that need, didn't matter.

"What have you got to lose, May?"

"My dignity. I would probably die of embarrassment being naked in front of everyone."

Cynthia sighed. "Listen. I know this would be hard but think about what you could gain from it. You could really find your sexual identity. Believe me, I know what you're feeling right now. I wondered why people were so bent on getting into bed with each other. Sex was horrible, more like a thing to endure. Then I met Chris."

A slight ping of jealousy hit May's heart. Cynthia's whole face softened, as did her voice.

"It was the first time I could say I enjoyed sex. And it was like a whole new world opened for me. I definitely would not have moved here. I probably would have married some Neanderthal my father picked out and kept wondering why the hell everyone was so excited about having sex."

"But you did that without an audience."

Cynthia fixed her with a stare. "I know this is scary. It's going to be hard enough if this is truly what you need. Not everyone understands the life. At least at the club you will never worry about being unacceptable." She leaned closer. "This could really change your life...and for the better."

It could. She felt it to her bones. There had always been something missing in sex, from the first time up until the last time a few months ago. She could feel the excitement, be ready to really get down to it, then she would get in bed. The embarrassment of those times, of never being fulfilled and having some of the guys, especially Rick, blame her was humiliating. Was that any worse than this? That had been in private at least. The public humiliation of Rick's accusations of her cheating on him still hurt. And worse, she had been in a way.

"What does Chris think?"

"Didn't ask him. He thinks of you as his little sister. While he has no trouble with me at the club, he might have a problem with his little sister going there, especially for this."

Did she really want to do this? While Cynthia thought there was a way out, that there would be a way for her to quit, there wouldn't. For May, if she was going to do this, she would go into it with full gusto.

"Okay. What do I need to do?"

"I'll call Micah. He wants a contract, and you have to have a physical."

May nodded, her body still tingling from the rush of heat.

Cynthia practically hopped up the stairs to Micah's office. She knew just what buttons to push, and while she felt a little guilty, she knew without a doubt that May needed this. She hurt each time she thought of her friend's embarrassed face and tortured voice whenever she talked of sex. Oh, when they were in the company of others, she would joke. But Cynthia knew she had suffered from not finding fulfillment.

She opened the door and smiled at Micah then turned her attention to her fiancé. He stood and she strode over to him and gave him an enthusiastic kiss.

"Well?" he asked.

"She'll do it."

"You're both crazy."

They turned and faced Micah.

"I think it will work out," Chris said. "Cynthia is sure she's a submissive, and Jesus, if anything, it will get Evan off his ass. He haunts my place anymore and it will get embarrassing." He looked at Cynthia. "Do you think there will be a problem?"

"No, and we had help from Evan."

Chris laughed. "What happened?"

"He came in giving her orders, telling her that he'd talked to that ex of hers about her car. Lord, that was the last thing he should have done."

"He's just trying to find out what happened."

Cynthia sighed. "Yeah, well, he's acting like a bull in a china shop. Either way, he told her she should make better choices in who she dates. It sent her over the edge."

"I bet."

"Chambers finds out about this, he isn't going to be happy," Micah said.

Micah hadn't been keen on the idea, but Cynthia knew it was the right thing to do.

"I'll take care of Evan," Chris said. "Just get the contract written up."

Micah nodded.

"I gotta get back to Dupree's."

They walked through the darkened club and Cynthia winced when Chris opened the door. She pulled out her sunglasses and slipped them on.

"You're sure about this?"Chris asked.

Without hesitating, she nodded. "Yes. One way or another, they have to move on. And even if Evan doesn't step in, May is a sub. She needs this. And what's more, I know exactly how she feels. I can't stand thinking she's suffering."

He wrapped his arms around her and pulled her into his warmth. She could smell the aftershave he used and the warm, delicious scent that was pure Chris Dupree. He kissed her on the nose. The love she saw in his gaze caused her heart to constrict. Would she ever get used to this man? Every day she was so blessed to have him.

The first stirrings of desire flickered through her blood. She frowned. "We have no time right now. I have interviews and you have to get back to work."

His smile widened. "But it's my early night, and I will definitely be in charge tonight."

The warmth boiled up and over into heat. "I'm counting on it."

May parked her car behind her brother's truck, happy to see he was home. Kai had been doing so much work lately that they hadn't had enough time together. Only thirteen months apart in age, they had always been close. But recently, with their schedules, they hadn't spent a lot of time together. It was as if they didn't even live in the same house. She slipped out of her car, smiling at the newly painted door. It had only taken a couple weeks to get it all straightened out, and now her car looked brand new.

Knowing that not one of the four men she lived with would have checked the mail, she slowly made her way over to the box. She slipped the key into the slot and opened it. As she walked to the front door, she could smell huhi huhi chicken. Ah, her father was grilling and that meant she didn't have to cook. The mail consisted of mainly bills and junk. There was one envelope addressed to her. It didn't look like a bill or junk so she dumped the rest of the mail on the table.

"Anyone around?"

Kai stuck his head around the corner. "We're all out back. Dad cooked."

She smiled. "I smelled it out front. I'm going to change and be out in a minute."

He saluted her and slipped back outside as she walked to her room. Pulling off her clothes, she sighed. She picked a T-shirt and a pair of yoga shorts, donned them, then grabbed up the letter again. She slipped her finger inside and tore it open. It contained one slip of paper and her blood froze when she opened it. In letters cut out from newspapers and magazines, it read:

You think you know everything, so smart, so fucking brilliant. People do not know what a two-faced bitch you are. I can't wait to see you fail, to see you hurt.

Her heart stuttered then ratcheted into a rhythm that would surely kill her. Her breath clogged her throat. Her vision dimmed and the room spun around her.

"May!" Kai yelled. His hands were on her, holding her up.

She shook her head, trying to clear the buzzing out of her

ears.

"May? Are you all right? Do I need to call Dad—"

The threat of bringing their father in brought her back from the edge. It was going to be bad enough once her family found out about the letter.

With quite an effort, she pulled herself together. "No. Give me a minute or two before calling Dad in."

She patted his hand and moved away from him toward the table. "It seems someone isn't too happy with me."

Kai followed her line of vision and his golden eyes darkened when he saw the letter. He moved to grab it, but she stopped him.

"No. My prints are all over it, so we need to keep it as clean as possible."

"Where did the bastard leave it?"

"He mailed it."

"Fuck."

"Exactly."

"You are going to call the police."

Not a question but a command. May had been planning on doing just that, but she did not like Kai's tone.

"Of course I am. What do you take me for?"

"I don't want you hedging on this. Rick can't keep getting away with this."

Her temper sparked. "How do you know it's him? I haven't heard from him since Chris banned him and threatened to have me file a restraining order. It has been months."

Kai shoved his hand through his short hair. "I don't know what you saw in him to begin with."

She settled her hands on her hips. "Oh, really? Why don't

you talk to Dad about it? He's the one who set us up."

"Well, he was definitely lacking, like most of the guys he finds for you. Why did you have to keep dating him?"

There was something in his voice she had not heard before. A disdain...or maybe an irritation. He took exception with some of the men she dated? He had a lot of nerve. "At least the guys I date have brains. They don't have them removed like the bimbos you date. Do you give them an IQ test to see if they are stupid enough or is it just luck?"

A snort sounded, then his shoulders started shaking. He turned to face her. "Just luck."

The tension drained. Her muscles relaxed, the twinkle in his eyes telling her Kai had irritated her on purpose. He knew if she was arguing with him, she wouldn't be so scared.

"Go get Dad, and I'll call HPD. We might as well get this over with."

"They still have no idea?" Chris asked after May told him the story the next morning.

She shook her head and leaned back in her chair. "No. The postmark isn't going to give them anything. They checked the prints. Mine are on there of course, and a few unidentified, but with the handling of the mail, who knows how many people touched it. None of them came up in their database though. So, whoever is doing this doesn't have a record. They're double checking with the post office about the finger prints of people who might have handled it there."

"Dammit. How did your father handle it?"

"Dad was okay, a little more serious about it than the car thing. Kai on the other hand was horrible. He insisted on driving me to work today."

Chris nodded. "I would do the same thing."

May rolled her eyes. "Of course you would."

He opened his mouth to respond when there was a knock at the door. Sheila, the new line cook stuck her head in. "Everyone is ready to discuss the new menu ideas."

"Be there in a second."

She nodded and shut the door. Chris switched his attention back to May. "I'm adding some extra security cameras. Also, Freddy is making sure there are some regular drive-bys on the nights you're working."

May wasn't going to argue. "That's fine. I just don't want it to become a distraction. Keeping everything normal is very important for me."

Chris cocked his head to one side. "I know it is, but that isn't the most important thing here. Keeping you safe is. Hopefully, HPD will find the bastard soon enough."

May nodded. "You better get to the meeting. I'm going to finish up these schedules."

"Will do. You made a good choice with Sheila. She's going to be good."

She smiled at him. "Of course she's wonderful. I hired her."

He laughed and squeezed her shoulder as he headed to the door. "Make sure to get something into your stomach before the dinner rush starts."

"Yes, sir."

"Why do you always sound like you're mocking me when you say that?"

She widened her eyes. "I have no idea, boss."

He was chuckling as he slipped out of the room, leaving her alone with the scheduling problems. Some of the servers had new class schedules and May needed to work around them. She scooted around the desk and set to work.

It wasn't until the door opened that she looked at the clock. Jeez, it was almost four-thirty. Chris would have a fit when he realized she hadn't eaten. She opened her mouth, ready to argue with him only to find Evan standing with his hand on the door knob.

"Uh...I thought Chris was working today."

"He had a meeting with Michael and the rest of the cooking staff. They're working on some ideas for new additions to the menu."

"Hmm." He stuck his hands in his pockets and continued to stare at her. The weight of his attention started to make her uncomfortable. She couldn't read the look on his face.

"Is there something you needed?"

"What?"

"Something you needed. From Chris."

He shook his head. "No. I just—"

"Excuse me." Sheila was tiny but she had a big voice. She slipped past Evan and May smiled when she saw the sandwich on the plate. "Boss said you needed to eat."

After setting the plate in front of May, she headed out, but not before she shot May thumbs up behind Evan's back.

"I guess I should let you get back to work."

His tone told her he didn't want to go, and of course, she didn't want him to go. The last few weeks had been strained, to say the least. Ever since their argument over Rick, they had spoken little, although Evan was here most nights she worked. She wanted to clear the air. She was in love with him, and she knew nothing would come of it. But more than that, she valued his friendship.

"No, I'm not really busy now and if I don't eat this monster sandwich that the boss made, he'll complain. You know how irritating he can be if he doesn't get his way."

Evan chuckled, the sound of it warming her blood. Damn, he had the sexiest chuckle, one she had dreamed of hearing as she lay next to him in bed.

"If you're sure."

She nodded as he took one of the seats in front of Chris's desk.

"I wanted to apologize."

She stopped in mid-chew and then swallowed. "You what?"

"I feel badly about embarrassing you."

"And?"

"That's it."

She sighed and set the sandwich down. "You aren't apologizing for your behavior with Rick?"

His jaw hardened as did his eyes. "Why do you care about him so much? He's slime."

"Yes. But that isn't what irritated me."

"You could have fooled me. You seem more concerned that I hit him than your own safety."

She pushed her sandwich away. Chris was just going to have to accept she couldn't finish it with Evan glaring at her.

"I wasn't worried about Rick. I was worried about you."

His eyes narrowed. "What do you mean?"

"Rick couldn't hurt you physically, and well, I'm sure you scared the living hell out of him, but he's petty. He might do something to hurt you...or your contracting business. I'd hate for that to happen."

For a second, he said nothing, and then he seemed to relax. "I can handle him. He might be a celebrity around here, but I've been here longer, have too many contacts."

"I was also mad that everyone was treating me like a little girl."

"I wasn't doing that. I was just trying to find out the truth."

"Why? The police had already talked to him, knew he had an alibi and you knew that too."

"It isn't that tight of an alibi."

"When I talked to Officer Carino last night—"

"Why were you talking to him? Did something happen?"

Damn. "Yeah. I got a letter in the mail."

"Fuck. At your house?"

She nodded, and she could admit to herself she was more than a little creeped out by it. "They're working on the fingerprints on the envelope but mine were the only ones they cleared. Anyway, Kai followed me to work. It isn't like I didn't take precautions."

"The letter, what did it say?"

She told him and he let loose a stream of profanity that was a little much, even for Evan.

"I called the police right away. They're looking into it."

Evan popped up out of his chair and started pacing. "But the bastard knows where you live."

"A lot of people do. I've lived there since I was two years old."

He waved that away. "It's taking it to the next level."

She nodded. "I agree. But—"

"I can't believe you didn't call me."

"What?"

"I mean, would it have killed you to let me know..." He stopped in midsentence, halted his pacing and looked at her.

"Never mind."

She frowned at him. "I wasn't alone. The whole family was home."

He settled his hands on his hips and nodded.

"I just want you to know that while appreciate your concern, I can take care of myself." He opened his mouth but she rolled ahead. "Keeping my life as normal as possible is important. This sicko would get some kind of thrill knowing he screwed with me. But don't think for a second I'm not taking this seriously. It hurts that so many people in my life, mainly the men, seem to think I'm an imbecile."

His expression softened. "You're one of the smartest women I know."

Heat filled her face and her heart skipped a beat. Everything in her felt giddy and just because he called her smart. Jesus. Was she that far gone over him? Would she never be able to move on? She cleared her throat.

"Thank you."

"I just want to make sure you're safe."

She nodded, unable to even speak. The sincerity in his voice had a lump forming in her throat. She might never be his type of woman, but there was no denying he did care about her. Evan had a truly big heart for his friends.

"I'll leave you alone about it if you promise me one thing."

"What?"

"Do you promise to let me know if anything else happens?" She didn't answer right away so he continued "I know I don't have a right to demand, but you're one of my best friends...my only female friend other than Cynthia. I just worry about you."

She relented because he didn't order her. "I will."

Something moved over his face but it was gone before she

could even decipher it.

"Thank you."

Silence filled the office as neither of them seemed to come up with anything to say. A second later, Evan's face flushed with...embarrassment? Jeez, she would have never thought she'd see Evan Chambers blush.

"I've gotta get going."

"Boss will probably be back in a second or two."

He shook his head as he backed up to the door. "I was just taking a breather before I head to Aeia to do an estimate. On a kitchen rehab. In a house."

She frowned at him. "Okay. I'll tell Chris you stopped by."

He nodded, then turned on his heel and practically ran out of the room.

She sighed as she looked down at the schedule and then grabbed her sandwich. The men in her life were going to drive her insane.

Chapter Six

May closed her eyes and allowed the techno beat of the club's music to pulse through her blood. Excitement skittered over her flesh as she tried her best to contain it. It might be her first time here, but she wanted to try her best not to look like a rookie.

"You know, you might enjoy the atmosphere a bit more if you open your eyes."

She did and slanted a look at her best friend. Cynthia's guileless blue eyes and innocent smile hid a very wicked mind and sometimes an even more wicked tongue.

Leaning over so she could shout in her ear, May said, "If I didn't owe you for getting me in here, I'd smack you upside the head, sistah."

Cynthia laughed and took a sip of her lava flow before answering. "You have to be nice to me. I won't take credit for the offer, since I think Micah came up with that." She shook her head. "Still, without me, you'd still be trying to figure out a way to come up with the five thousand dollar joining fee."

That much was true. Rough 'n Ready was Honolulu's premier BDSM club and it did have a hefty price tag to ensure the patrons were serious about their lifestyle. May wasn't poor. Chris paid her a good price to manage Dupree's, but she also didn't have money like that to throw around.

"That much we can agree on." She looked around and noticed they'd lost Chris somewhere along the way. "What happened to your better half?"

"He's talking to Micah. I still can't believe you agreed to a public submission."

"You're the one who talked me into it."

Cynthia laughed. "I know, but I am still surprised."

May glanced toward the area where many of the people where gathered. She hadn't seen it up close, but she knew there were glass squares that allowed patrons a front-row seat to the D/s play going on in the rooms below. The participants choose whether or not to allow the audience to see the session.

She shivered thinking of all those people watching her. She hadn't completely come to terms with what she needed and she'd agreed to her first true session in front of a flipping audience. Crazy, or as her grandfather would say, *pupule.* She couldn't contain the dueling emotions as they flooded her. Fear with a healthy dose of arousal and excitement fought for control and she was amazed she hadn't gone completely *pupule* from the battle beneath the surface.

The desire to know more about herself, what she needed, was the only thing keeping her in the club. It wasn't until she started talking to Cynthia a few months earlier that May realized why she might be bored in the bedroom. She hadn't slept with a lot of men, but she'd had enough lovers to know she was missing something. With a little research, she'd come to understand why she found most of her sexual partners lacking.

She shook herself out of her thoughts and studied the customers. There were a few faces she recognized, including one of the former line cooks from Dupree's. It was crowded as she assumed it was every Saturday night, but she understood it was busy every night of the week. Most clubs like it were little more than meat markets. They played at being BDSM clubs, but they weren't serious. They didn't have the strict security guidelines Micah insisted on or the hefty joiner's fee. Rough 'n Ready required a thorough background check for security. That made the other clubs not only subpar, but also potentially dangerous.

She glanced at her friend. "I didn't have much choice. It was that or pay the five thousand. I just can't spare that amount of money."

Cynthia nodded. "I know, but...when I was starting out in this world, I wouldn't have had the nerve to do it, not in a public forum. Of course, I don't have your fantasy of exhibitionism."

"Really?" May faced Cynthia. "I'd never guess you had any second thoughts."

"I did. And third, fourth... You get the idea." She shrugged. "Thank God for Chris, because I was really out of my depth. And seriously, I probably would have never made that leap if it hadn't been for him."

Something caught Cynthia's attention over May's shoulder. A second later, her whole face lit up with a smile and May knew who she'd seen. She couldn't fight the little twinge of envy that curled in her gut. Twisting around, she watched Chris make his way through the crowd. He kept getting interrupted along the way, and being the ultimate businessman, he stopped, smiled and chatted.

It gave her time to study the man with him, who she assumed was Micah. Taller than Chris by an inch or two, he probably outweighed him by fifty pounds—all muscle. Long, silky black hair spilled over his shoulders, a testament to his Native American background, as were the high cheekbones and strong jaw.

"He's pretty, isn't he?" Cynthia asked.

Without taking her attention away from Micah, she nodded. His lips where full, sensuous, and even looking as irritated as he did now, he was gorgeous. The light was dim, but she could see the reddish gold tone to his skin. He stood out from the mostly leather-clad patrons due to his stature and his clothing. A dark blue dress shirt fit snugly over his impressive chest and the casual dress slacks hugged his lean hips. It wasn't what May expected the owner of a BDSM club to wear, especially at work.

"I hate to say it, because it probably sounds bad, but all I can think of when I see him is a conquering warrior," Cynthia said.

Again, May didn't take her gaze away from the man who was now impatiently looking around the club. She wished she could see the shade of his eyes. They weren't black, or even brown, but something lighter.

When his eagle gaze zeroed in on her, she froze. The frown wrinkling his brow cleared, and one side of his mouth quirked. Touching two fingers to his forehead, he gave her a salute. Heat ping-ponged through her belly and her heart skipped a beat.

May licked her lips. "Oh, that is one dangerous man, sistah."

Cynthia laughed. "Yeah and you just agreed to submit to him to get in his club."

"Holy Lord, what was I thinking?" She barely whispered the words, so not even Cynthia could hear her. Before she could come to terms with Micah and just what she'd agreed to, another man, one who used to make her knees go weak and her body vibrate with lust, stepped into view beside the club owner.

"What the hell is Evan doing here?"

Cynthia stepped up beside her and cocked her head. "He probably comes here most weekends."

Both women watched as Evan and Micah started arguing, Evan doing most of the shouting as the other man said little.

"That's odd. I always thought they were on friendly terms. Evan is considered one of the top Doms, and Micah does like the way he draws a crowd when he performs."

May glanced at Cynthia whose frown deepened. "Oh, crap. Now Chris is getting into the middle of it." With one last gulp of her drink, she set it down on a nearby table and grabbed May's hand. "Let's go smooth some male egos."

Evan Chambers strode through Rough 'n Ready, searching for Chris Dupree while various scenarios of hurting his best friend flitted through his mind. All of them included an extreme amount of pain and degradation.

What the fuck is Chris thinking bringing May to a place like this, let alone setting her up for public display? She didn't belong in a BDSM club anymore than Evan belonged at a monastery. Even that ridiculous image couldn't cool his temper. Nothing would until he had it out with Chris.

Violence bubbled in his blood as he brushed past the milling patrons. When he spotted Chris chatting to Micah, Evan's anger surged. Evan changed directions and headed straight for them, ignoring more than one person as he practically plowed his way to where they stood.

He ordered himself to calm down, to control his fury as he neared the two men, but as he thought of what he'd been told, a red haze filled his vision and he lost the ability to think straight.

"What the fuck are you thinking bringing May here?" Evan shouted.

"Well, good evening to you, Evan," Chris said, then calmly sipped his drink.

"I don't have time for this shit. What the hell are you doing?"

"I was talking to Micah." He gestured toward his partner.

Evan felt his grip on his temper slipping. "Why did you bring May here? And what is this crap about her having a public submission to gain her membership?"

"She told Cynthia she wanted to see what the club was like," Chris said. "How did you find out about it?"

"Jay told me the moment I walked through the door." Evan scowled, thinking of the way the bouncer had licked his lips when he told him about it. "It's probably all over the fucking club by now."

"Hell." Chris heaved a sigh and shrugged. "There's nothing that can be done now."

"It isn't like they wouldn't figure it out soon enough." Micah's calm voice sent another surge of rage coursing through Evan's veins.

He glanced at his friend who stood there in the middle of the most decadent club on the island, looking as if he were discussing the weather.

"And just what the hell are you thinking? Taking on a rookie sub? Hell, I can't remember the last time you performed for a crowd."

"What does it matter to you, Chambers?" Again Micah's cool, composed tone set his annoyance soaring.

"May's a friend and she just isn't the kind of girl for something like this." He ground his teeth together and bit out every word. "Definitely not for public display. And with her recent problems, I would think something like this would be ill advised."

"Hello, boys." Cynthia's sultry southern voice lifted above the music and the clashing male egos.

Evan glanced over her and frowned. Petite and curvy, Evan noticed Cynthia had definitely dressed for the club tonight. It wasn't often Chris's fiancé wore all black, but when she did, she stood out. She smiled at Evan.

"Looks like you're having a bit of a problem. Is there something we can do to help?"

Evan didn't miss the sparkle in her eyes that told him she knew exactly what the argument had been about. A switch like Chris, Cynthia understood the ramifications of what May had agreed to and should have protected her. He didn't feel like fighting with her right now. Besides, there was a good chance Chris would kick his ass if he did.

"No, there isn't anything you can do other than get May out of here."

He dismissed her without another word and ignored her amused snort. Instead, he turned his attention to the woman causing the irritation.

Maylea Aiona was the kind of woman you took home to Mama, that is if you had one. Since the day he met her, May had been like the little sister he'd never had. Okay, not really. There was a moment or two...or maybe three that he'd thought of how it would feel to have all that black, silky hair tickle his chest as she worked her way down to his cock.

He shifted his weight, trying to relieve the sudden pressure in his groin. That one image had been haunting his dreams—not to mention his daytime hours—for the past few months. With the way she was dressed now, he knew they'd be worse tonight. The snug black sleeveless top accentuated her full breasts, showing just enough cleavage to entice. The skirt was long, leather and black and from the attention she got walking toward them, he was sure it hugged that wonderfully rounded ass she had.

"Is there a problem?" May asked. Her lyrical voice held a hint of sass that he'd come to love. Evan sometimes would sit near her stand at Dupree's just to hear her talk. And laugh. God Almighty the woman had a sexy laugh.

He cleared his throat and tried to ignore the way his blood rushed to his shaft. "Yeah, something's wrong."

She frowned at him, her brow wrinkling and confusion darkening her Caribbean blue eyes.

Chris made a sound of disgust that caused her to break her gaze from Evan's.

"Nothin's wrong, May. Evan is going all big brother and saying Micah never should've offered a membership to you on the terms he did."

Before Evan could break in and voice his opinions, Micah stepped forward. He took May's hand and, leaning closer than Evan thought he needed to, he said, "Since no one here seems to have manners, I'll introduce myself. Micah Ross, owner of this fine establishment. You must be Maylea Aiona."

May, damn her, smiled shyly at Micah. "Yes. I can't thank you enough for this."

Micah placed his hand over hers. "The pleasure will be all mine, I'm sure."

An emotion Evan didn't want to examine too closely had him fighting the urge to grab May by the wrist and drag her hand away from Micah, and then pull her out of the club. He knew her well enough to know she would skin him alive if he embarrassed her that way.

"Listen, I hate to break this up, but I'm disagreeing to your contract with May."

Micah looked up at him, his straight, clear gaze showing no surprise. "You're telling me what I can do?"

It was a direct question that most of the people standing around watching them wouldn't understand. Not many people knew of his silent partnership with Micah. Evan hadn't intruded on the everyday running of the club—until now.

"I am. I can't trust you with her."

One ebony eyebrow shot up, but the self-satisfied smirk confused Evan. "Interesting." He returned his attention to May. "I'm sorry but it seems that Evan is objecting to my agreement."

May's spine stiffened inch by inch. Pulling her hand out of Micah's grasp, she scowled back over her shoulder at Evan. Fire snapped in her eyes and her skin flushed with anger. Damn, she even looked sexy when she was pissed off.

"This isn't any of your damned business. And besides, I signed a contract, went through all the background checks and even had a thorough exam." She twisted back around to face Micah. "Unless you want it known you failed to meet your obligations. And believe me, one little word from me, and you *will* have problems, bruddah."

Micah looked as if he were fighting not to laugh but used the same pleasant tone. "What it says is that you must publically submit to an owner of the club."

"Yeah. So, if you renege I'll make your life hell."

A sinking feeling enveloped Evan as he watched Micah raise his gaze again. The music has shifted from pulse-pounding rock to something bluesy and sultry, but Evan barely noticed it above the roaring in his head. Even knowing what Micah was about to say, he didn't accept it until his friend opened his mouth.

"Since Evan disagrees with the idea of me being the Dom tonight, maybe he can fill the role."

His body reacted immediately. His cock thumped against the zipper of his jeans and his heart pounded against his chest. This was heaven and hell all rolled into one little bundle. He knew his choice. Either he agreed to Micah's challenge, or he had to allow Micah to touch her, break her. He could imagine a woman as strong willed as May being a challenge to any Dom, but Micah played it right up to the edge of the rules. Since those rules were his own, Micah rarely went over that line, but he got damned close to it. Evan refused to let his partner even think about putting his hands on May.

Evan didn't look at May when he nodded, sealing his fate. Something that might have been disappointment flashed in Micah's eyes before he looked away.

"What?" May's outraged shriek turned even more heads and irritated Evan. She didn't need to sound so horrified.

"I'm sorry darlin' but that's the choice you have. Unless you want to change your mind and give up the session," Evan said.

She crossed her arms beneath her breasts and pursed her lips. Evan knew that pose well enough. May was pissed, but she was also plotting. That could have disastrous results.

"You said it had to be an owner."

Micah nodded in Evan's direction. "Meet the silent partner of Rough 'n Ready."

She turned, her eyes rounded in horror. "Tell me this isn't true."

Evan shrugged. "You can give the idea up, which I think you should."

As soon as he said the words, he realized his mistake. Telling May what to do always got her back up. She shivered, her whole body moving with the motion. "No. And if I have to do it with you, I want it over as soon as possible."

Damn. She sounded as if she were getting ready for the electric chair. Her unhappiness aggravated him. They'd had an easy relationship since he met her two years ago. Tonight would change all that, and he would truly regret the loss of her friendship. She was one of the few women he truly admired for her hard work and dedication to her family. But there would be no way he could touch her tonight and go back to being friends.

He needed her friendship. It was one of the bright spots of his day when he talked to her, teased her. He had to give it one more try.

"If this ever got back to your father, he'd be furious."

Her eyes narrowed and she tossed her hair over her shoulder. "And what are you going to tell him, Evan? 'Oh, Mr. Aiona, by the way, I stripped your daughter and made her submit to me in public.'" She snorted. "Yeah, I can see that going over really well."

Evan couldn't respond. The image of what she'd just said popped into his mind and all the remaining blood headed south to his shaft. He could just imagine how she'd looked strapped to his bed, her body flushed with excitement, begging him for completion. His mouth went dry thinking of how it would feel to slide the flat of his tongue over her copper brown nipple. Not to mention sinking lower, pressing his mouth to her sex, tasting her, devouring her.

"Ha!"

Her voice brought him out of his fantasy with a jolt. He shook his head, trying to lose the image he'd conjured.

"I knew you wouldn't have an answer to that, bra. Daddy would castrate you on the spot."

That damn mouth of hers was going to be a problem. "You

act odd for a woman who agreed to do this. Do you think you're up to it?"

Another mistake. It seemed to be a night for them. May thrived on challenges. And, even knowing that, understanding that this would ruin their friendship, he couldn't seem to stop himself.

"No problem. I can handle it. Can you?"

His inner warrior who had been clawing at his throat revolted at the thought. He should resist. It would be best just to grab her and drag her out of here. But he couldn't. He wanted to touch, to sample, to know what she sounded like when she came. The need humming in his veins took over all rational thought.

"Do you actually think you're up to it? Being stripped naked in front of a crowd of strangers? Are you ready to be watched as you lose yourself in submission?" he grated out.

Closing her eyes, she shivered, her body apparently reacting to the image he'd painted. *Damn.*

"I think you might regret pushing me, May."

She smiled and leaned forward, her eyes glittering with challenge. And damned if his cock didn't rise up and cheer.

"Prove it."

He studied her for a moment as everything and everyone around them faded into the background. It was inevitable, at least since he'd walked through the door of the club tonight. There was no way he'd let Micah handle her, and May's single-mindedness wouldn't let this go. He couldn't stop the excitement at the idea of taking her through the paces of her first submission. He wasn't good enough for her, never would be. If he couldn't stop this train wreck, at least he could be there for her. The emotional upheaval she was about to go through wouldn't be easy.

Evan motioned toward one of the subs.

When she reached the group, he said, "Take Ms Aiona to my room." He leaned closer so that only she could hear him. "Only females are allowed in the room. No other men are to touch her, understood?"

She nodded.

"Use the soft restraints and the coconut scented oil. I want it all over." As he instructed her, he had to bite back a groan. Just the thought of all that golden brown skin slick with oil had his balls aching. "Before she's undressed, I want her blindfolded."

The sub nodded again but she said nothing in response. She approached May. Only then did she lift her head. "If you'll follow me, Ms. Aiona?"

With one more furious glance that included both him and Micah, May followed the petite blonde through the milling customers. He watched the two of them walk away. His gaze zeroed in on May's ass. He'd been right about the skirt. It hugged her curves. He couldn't stop the sigh of appreciation. Once she was out of his sight, he turned to his partner.

"The office. Now." He didn't even wait for an agreement from Micah. As he walked past Chris, he said, "And don't even think of showing up. I'm not in the mood for your smirking face."

He pushed his way through the crowd, his mind jumbled with flashes of his fantasy come to life. May was a woman who didn't belong in a place like this. She shouldn't even know about it. And now, because of Cynthia and her damned interference, he was going to lose the one woman he considered a good friend.

He stomped up the stairs and glanced behind him. Micah had been detained by a female customer. Evan caught his eye and Micah nodded, letting him know he would follow him up.

Evan finished his ascent and pushed into the office, his rage still shimmering. What the hell were they all thinking? Had a steady relationship really caused Chris to lose all rational thought? May wasn't the type of woman who submitted. She was too bold, too...controlling. She could never live the life he did. It had to be the lure of the forbidden, the temptation to sin. Too many people thought they wanted a life like this and one trip told them it wasn't what they thought it was.

The office door swung open and Micah filled the entrance. He smiled with so much arrogance that Evan curled his fingers into his palms to keep from wrapping them around the bastard's neck.

"Let's have it, Chambers."

As Micah swaggered to his desk and dropped down in the chair, Evan rose, fighting the need to jump across the desk and punch his friend.

Evan drew in a deep breath, his head pounding, his body aching for a fight. From behind clenched teeth, he asked, "Give me one good reason not to kick your ass."

Chapter Seven

With pleasure, Micah watched his business partner and friend pace back and forth in front of his desk. When Chris had come to him with this idea, Micah'd never thought it'd work. Part of him was sure that Chris might be too caught up in love to realize not everyone had a soul mate. He'd expected Evan to shrug and order a drink. He was a cold bastard and little got beneath his steely control. But apparently one Hawaiian flower by the name of Maylea had.

"I can't believe you agreed to this. It's not like you at all." Anger vibrated in Evan's voice, but there was a hint of outright panic there too. He ran his hands through his hair, leaving his usually styled golden blond hair ruffled.

Damn, he was going to owe Chris fifty bucks over the bet. Evan was attracted to May, and not in his usual way. His behavior spoke of a deeper feeling. Evan was never truly possessive of anyone...until now.

"You've never complained about the way I ran the club before. In fact, you usually thank me for the good revenue, which I assure you will triple for tonight because of your upcoming performance."

A growl emanated from Evan's throat. He stopped in front of Micah's desk, planted his hands on the surface and leaned over with a menacing scowl. Fury clouded his eyes. "Don't you even think about using her to make fucking money."

The threat behind the words was clear—not to mention real. Evan vibrated with unleashed violence, something Micah hadn't seen in a good long while. At least not since they were both living on the streets of Atlanta. He knew from experience that fucking with Evan Chambers could really be painful.

"Take it easy. She wants this."

With a snort of disgust, Evan whirled away and started pacing again. "What the hell does she know? She's barely older than a high school senior."

Micah wanted to laugh, but he was pretty sure Evan would likely punch him. The bastard had a mean right hook. "I read her application, did the background check on her. She's twenty-five, and amazingly, not a virgin."

The look Evan shot him told Micah he would gladly strangle him for that last bit of info.

"I think you have some kind of notion of who she is and it's not even close to the mark."

Evan opened his mouth, but Micah held up his hand to forestall his argument.

"She's done her research. Shit, from what Chris says she has a photographic mind and can recite some passages word for word. I get the impression that she's been searching for this for awhile. It might not be what she wants in the end, but she doesn't strike me as an impulsive woman."

With an irritated sigh, Evan dropped into the chair in front of his desk, running his hands down the front of his jeans. Instead of looking at Micah, his attention was glued to the monitor in the room where they prepared May.

"No, she's not. That's why this makes no sense. I'd peg her as a control freak. She's run her family since she was twelve.

Hell, Chris made her manager when she was barely old enough to drink. And now, the place would fall apart without her if she were gone."

Micah studied him and realized that this was deeper than attraction. He couldn't put his finger on it, but in the twenty years they'd known each other, Micah hadn't seen Evan pay attention to a woman longer than a month, tops. And none of them had seemed to twist him inside out.

"Evan." He waited for his friend to look at him before speaking again. "You know the person we show the world is not always who we need to be in the bedroom."

He nodded once. "I know. But, she's—"

"She's a woman, just like the hundreds of women who are out there tonight. An adult who has decided she might want to try something new and exciting. If you're having second thoughts, just let me know. Teaching her a little submissiveness will be a pleasure, I assure you. I do love a sub with spunk."

Evan snarled at him and popped out of the chair. Before Micah could react, Evan had him by the collar of his shirt. He brought his face close to Micah's. Murder darkened his eyes. The last time Micah had seen that particular look, they'd both ended up with broken bones. "Don't fuck with me, Micah. I know where all your skeletons are buried."

Evan tossed him back in the chair and left without another word, slamming the door on his way out. Micah smiled, even if it did hurt. He hadn't been lying about his interest in the woman. The moment he saw her through the dim light of the club, he'd been half-aroused. He hated subs who relinquished to a Dom easily.

Turning his attention to May, he watched as the blindfold was slipped over her eyes. He recognized the mulish expression that passed over her face and chuckled. She wasn't going to say no, but she didn't like it.

Evan was right about her personality. She was a dominant on the outside, but from her application he knew she'd had problems in the bedroom. Men who were attracted to her would want her to take the lead, and she didn't want that.

Micah switched his focus to Evan as he made his way through the club. His determined trek through the throng of patrons reminded Micah of a soldier off to do battle.

His door opened almost silently. Without looking, he knew it was Chris.

"You were right."

"I know," Chris said, with a fair amount of smugness.

Micah slanted him a look. "I'm not sure it was the right thing to do. He's very pissed right now."

"Evan will control it. He always does."

"Which is not a good thing. But this could break him."

Chris settled in the chair that Evan had just vacated. "It won't, believe me. He can't ever move on from his need to control every little thing in his life until he confronts all his problems. His mother's memory taints every woman he looks at. Man needs to learn to trust."

"You've been spending too much time with your woman. You're starting to sound like Dr. Phil."

Chris laughed. "You're just jealous."

He nodded. "Of you because you have Cynthia, you're damn right." He looked at the monitor where May was shown again. "And who wouldn't be jealous of having her."

Chris froze. "Don't tell me you want her?"

Micah shrugged. "You know I like the subs with a little spark."

92

"Micah."

Micah said nothing for a good long while. "Don't worry, *Mommy*, I'd never step in unless asked. Just remember, if you're wrong, if she's not the one for him, he's going to be even more fucked up."

"Is that possible?"

He looked Chris in the eye feeling older than his thirty-five years, the weight of his own memories smothering him. "Believe me, it can be much worse." He stood, shaking away his memories, his pain.

Chris shook his head. "You've become a worrier. Let it go. I'm going to find something else to do while this goes on. I'm sure you don't want to miss the show, but I definitely don't want to even imagine it."

May released a sigh of pleasure as the sub's hands worked the scented oil over her skin. She'd been tense since Bianca had slipped the blindfold over her eyes. The silence had unnerved her but not as much as not knowing who was removing her clothes. She was pretty sure they were women. Their hands were small and she smelled perfume, not cologne.

Once she was naked, her arms had been pulled over her head. Cuffs made of soft, padded material were slipped over her hands and attached to what she assumed was the hook she had seen up on the ceiling. That done, at least two people were left, one in front and the other in back. They were slowly torturing her.

She bit her lower lip to keep from moaning as someone's hands slipped up and over the fullest part of her buttocks and traced a finger between her cheeks. She curled her toes against the cold platform of the dais.

It was bad enough she still couldn't wrap her mind around

the fact that Evan was going to be her Dom. She'd been prepared for Micah, for someone she didn't know to handle her as if she were just another woman. Fear and anticipation beat in her heart as she thought about what was to come.

The person in front of her paused before pouring more heated oil over her chest. Hands glided over the tops of her breasts, working the oil into her flesh. Fingers slipped between her breasts, then circled her nipples that were already unbearably sensitive.

She had never thought to have a woman's hands on her this way. May knew she wasn't attracted to them, but they did know just how to touch her. Soft hands glided over her skin and without the being able to see, she allowed herself to just feel.

She couldn't stop the moan as the woman in front skimmed her hand down May's stomach. Every nerve throbbed, her pussy clenching in reaction. Her whole body urged the unknown woman's hand down to her sex to offer relief. Knowing the rules, she said nothing, but she wanted to yell at them. She needed just a little stroke, one little touch and she would come.

As soon as the woman's hand reached her abdomen, the door slid open. Turning her head toward the sound, she sensed a difference in the room's atmosphere. Both subs dropped their hands from her, making her want to scream in frustration.

"Very good work, ladies. I do like it when my sub is wet and waiting." Evan's deep, southern voice caused her heart to slip down to her stomach. "Continue on."

It had been weeks that she'd been planning this, or something like it. Having Evan act as Dom added another level of fear and excitement to the whole process. Both women continued to stroke, massage, entice as Evan moved about the room. She heard a drawer open and shuffling followed. Soon, silence filled the room. Without sight she couldn't even sense what was going on now.

"Ladies, I think I can handle this by myself." When he spoke, she realized he hadn't moved far from the door.

She could sense they weren't happy with their dismissal, but they went as ordered. He murmured something to them she couldn't hear, but the door soon closed behind them with an audible click.

Evan approached her almost silently. He said nothing, but as he drew closer, she scented his musky cologne. Stepping up on the dais, he circled then stopped behind her. She could feel the heat of his body warming her back. His breath feathered across her shoulder and she couldn't fight the shiver. She started when he ran his finger across her stomach. A rush of tingles followed the path his fingers took. The teasing touch was just enough to drive her insane.

"Are you ready to submit?"

Chapter Eight

Evan drew in a deep breath and mentally counted backwards from ten. Just feeling her smooth bronze skin beneath his fingers was enough to make him come. The scent of coconut rose from her flesh. He licked his lips. He knew he had an audience, knew he had to keep it simple, but not since his first public session had he been this nervous. His palms were damp and his mouth was dry. His heart pumped, pushing blood so fast through his system he was amazed he could still stand up straight.

From the moment he'd walked into the room he'd been in tune with her. It happened sometimes with subs. Some basic primal connection where he knew what she needed. It had never been this strong, and definitely not before the first submission. It usually took several sessions. The instant bond he'd felt for May shocked him, aroused him.

It disturbed him enough just seeing her naked. He'd imagined her naked, what man wouldn't. She had one of those curvy bodies that made most men itch to touch, to explore, but he'd never imagined he would get to see her in the flesh. Granted, she'd starred in some extremely arousing dreams over the past couple of years. But nothing, not even his most vivid fantasies had gotten close to the reality.

The oil added a layer of sheen to her flesh, making it almost glow. Every loving inch of her was golden brown. Pretty, delectable dark brown nipples crowned her full, high breasts. When he saw her bare sex, he almost lost it. From the top of her head to the pretty pink toenails, she was his wet dream come to life.

Evan shifted closer and smiled when he heard her hitched breathing. Good, she wasn't so immune to him. He'd hoped she wasn't because it might make this easier. At least for her. For him...well, it would be painful. The joy that came from touching her would be equal to the torture from never being able to quench his thirst for her. This was about her submission, her satisfaction, there would be no completion for him.

He skimmed his hand up her torso and cupped the underside of her breast. His fingers itched to tease, pinch, but he knew it was too early. Stretching out the pleasure, building the anticipation—that made the submission so much more enjoyable for both of them.

"Micah tells me you've been researching." Even to his own ears his voice sounded like gravel. Lust and want had him by the balls. Thank God, she didn't know. He hoped.

"Yes."

He removed his hand in retribution. "I didn't ask. You don't talk unless given permission."

She said nothing, telling him that she understood. Oh, Evan was sure she longed to tear into him, but her willingness to go through with this was more important. It was that tenacity in her nature that had always drawn him to her.

Wanting to reward her, he moved her hair aside and skimmed his hand down her delicate spine. A tattoo of a hibiscus decorated the small of her back, just above her full, rounded ass. He'd caught glimpses of it when she'd worn shorter shirts, but seeing it completely unobstructed was different. Evan yearned to linger, to trace his finger over the intricate design. The audience above made that impossible. He resented them, resented that the one time his dream would be within reach, he had to perform in front of them.

He rested his hand on her hip before speaking again. "I know you've read the rules, but I want to go over them just in case. You do not speak unless I ask. You are under my control. All your thoughts, your actions, your pleasure, are for me to give. Do you understand?"

"Yes."

Her immediate compliance twisted his gut and sent a fresh jolt of electric lust careening through his blood. Reminding himself this was just one act, without the possibility of a follow-up, didn't matter. His body reacted anyway. He'd probably have the imprint of his zipper on his cock for a week. "And do you have a safe word, something that will tell me I might have gone too far?"

"Aloha."

He couldn't fight the curving of his lips. May was thoroughly modern, but she loved her Hawaiian roots.

With an extra squeeze to her hip, Evan moved toward the toy selection he'd laid out on the table. He picked up the paddle, running the soft padded leather over his free hand. It was one of his favorite toys because he knew from experience it heightened a sub's pleasure with the minimum of pain. While he did participate in D/s, he didn't get off on pain. He liked the mental complexities of it, and he liked to tease his sub. Sensations, not pain, were more important to him. Although it varied from sub to sub.

As he approached her, Evan's heart skipped. He didn't think he would ever get the image of her out of his head. It would be stamped so deep in his psyche, he would probably dream about it for the rest of his life.

With a deep breath, he continued until he stood in front of the platform. He placed the items on the edge then walked up the steps slowly.

Evan stood in front of her, breathing in her scent. Sweet coconut. Rich, musky aroused woman. He looked down at her oiled nipples glistening under the lights. He didn't resist the impulse to brush the backs of his fingers over the tight buds. She sucked in a breath and shuddered, her breasts swaying slightly with the motion. God Almighty, he was going to die from lack of blood to his brain. He slipped his fingers up and over and traced the outer edge of her areolas. She pulled her bottom lip between her teeth as she visibly drew her reaction in.

"There are no rules against showing your pleasure. It will help me understand what you want...need from me."

He rolled one nipple between his fingers. A low moan escaped. "That's good."

With one last soft pinch to each nipple, he released her and unhooked the restraints from the ceiling. Rubbing his hands down her arms, he led her toward the middle of the platform. A crinkle formed above her eyes telling him she was confused. While some Doms got off on keeping a sub completely in the dark, and it did have its place in some training, a new sub needed to know the basics to ease their nerves. Anticipation was one thing, being skittish was another thing all together.

"I don't like leaving anyone in that position for too long. It's not good for the circulation, and it really isn't the ideal position for what I had in mind."

Evan couldn't keep the excitement or need out of his voice. He wasn't sure she could recognize it. His body screamed to conquer, to take her as his, but he knew it wouldn't happen. It was his job to initiate her, nothing else. The idea that he would never touch her after tonight ate at him He led her down the stairs to one of his favorite pieces of equipment. Shaped like a gymnasium horse, it could be lowered in height and provided hooks on the side for her restraints. He still said nothing, knowing that the silence added a level of tension that would bring her a more glorious release in the end.

Without a word, he pressed on her lower back, urging her forward. Soon he had her bent over, her cuffs hooked on, and her ass in the perfect position for the ultimate viewing experience for the audience. He'd made sure the audio had been turned off for them, although he knew that had not been Micah's intention. But he wanted music for the two of them, just for them. After he picked out his favorite playlist, one that always reminded him of May, the smooth, sensual voice of Lauryn Hill filled the room. He moved the paddle into grabbing distance.

Not being able to resist, he placed both hands on the fullest part of her ass and squeezed. She rarely wore jeans or pants to work, so seeing the actual shape of her rear didn't happen that often. Still, it wouldn't matter after tonight. Every time he closed his eyes he would probably see it. Lord knows he'd dream of taking her from behind. He slid his hands up and over to the small of her back. His fingers trembled and he had to grit his teeth to fight the desire to slip them between her cheeks, into the small puckered hole. She tensed slightly. With one last lingering caress, he moved to pick up the paddle.

"I glanced at your questionnaire." He rubbed the padded toy over her rear end. "You seem to have a...shall we call it...*interest* in spankings."

May sucked in a quick breath as she tried to calm her racing heart. When she'd filled out the application she had been completely honest. In this, she wanted to be true to herself, or she would never find out just what was wrong with her in the bedroom. But everything had spiraled out of control when Evan had stepped in as her Dom. She knew he thought he was protecting her in some way, but it had added another layer of excitement to it all. She hadn't expected the stakes to rise to this level so fast. At least, that was what she was thinking. What she was feeling...well, it overrode any objections her mind might have.

Every nerve in her body was attuned to Evan. This went beyond infatuation—*that* she had dealt with for the past few years and had been positive she'd shaken the affliction. No, this was scarier, more uncontrollable. This encompassed her entire being.

With the blindfold shielding her eyes, she could hear his every move, even with the music pumping through the speakers. Each shift of his feet made her pulse jump. Heat surged through her blood and her heart smacked against her ribs. She yearned to feel his hands on her again. There was a gentleness in his caress she hadn't expected for a man who was always so hard. She worried about her mind while her body craved his touch—but she did her best not show any of this. She knew this was a game, to see if he could control her. While she knew that at some point she would have to give in a little, she would be damned if she would relinquish everything to a man who would never see her as a woman. He acted as if she was some non-sexual being, that her needs should be pure or nonexistent. That was, until tonight. Now, he wanted to fulfill her fantasies. And, dammit, that pissed her off.

He drew closer and she could smell his cologne. Musky, sandalwood, it was the same it had always been. But there was something different beneath it, something that attracted her more. Taking another deep breath, she realized it was Evan. It was his unique wild scent that tantalized her. She tried to swallow but found her mouth dry.

He tapped her rear end with the paddle. Just a swat—barely that—but her breathing hitched and her chest grew tight. Still she tried her best not to show her reaction. Evan rubbed it against her rear again and without warning, pulled back and smacked her. This time though, it was harder. Heat vibrated from that spot outward. With the next hit, her sex clenched as she grew damp. May used every ounce of her self-control to resist the urge to rub against the contraption she was tethered to. Before she could recover, he gave her another slap, again a little harder than the last. *Holy mother of God.* Just those few slaps had liquid heat filling her sex. She curled her toes and waited for the next smack. He said nothing, but she could hear him breathing, sense him standing behind her.

Seconds ticked by. The music changed to something slower, sultrier. It was a man this time singing of seduction and love. She wanted to move, to ease the tension, but the silence stretched, as did her nerves. When Evan finally touched her, he used his hand, smoothing over the irritated spot he'd smacked. Heated skin met cool palm. His fingers danced over her flesh, leaving the already sensitized area tingling.

"Your skin pinkens so nicely."

His voice had deepened along with his southern accent. She had always loved his twang, the way it slipped over the words, drew out the endings. But now, it was even more pronounced. It made her think of lounging in bed, his hands leisurely coursing over her flesh.

A moment later, it was as if he had read her mind. He traced between her cheeks, his callused digits barely touching her flesh. Every instinct urged her to rise to her tiptoes and invite him to slip between her cheeks, but she fought it. Evan might want her to show her pleasure, but she knew the game. If she exposed any weakness to him, he would use it to get to her. And dammit, she refused to do that. It was bad enough he was the one she was submitting to. She refused to let him break her. She knew if he had been Micah, she wouldn't have fought it like this, but something about having Evan as her Dom made her want to be more defiant. Instead of stopping, Evan skimmed his fingers between her legs to her swollen sex. Just one touch of his fingers to her slit and she quivered. The area was already sensitive from her anticipation. The spanking had heightened her arousal, had her dripping. Her clit was hard, aching, ready to be caressed into orgasm. Curling her lips inward, she fought any sound that threatened to escape. She was ready to come if he would just move the tip of his finger a little higher...

She couldn't stop the moan that escaped the moment he moved his hand away. Masculine satisfaction filled his chuckle.

"Don't worry. Your time is near. But I get the sense you think you decide what happens."

She was more than willing to give him a piece of her mind and she tried to jerk her head around to tell him, but he stayed her with his hand. His fingers slipped through her silky hair, almost as if he was trying to calm her. He massaged her scalp with tender strokes. Damn him, it was working. The arousal was still there, still had her tense, but when he was touching her she could somehow find a bit of peace. He bent down until his face was level with hers.

"Easy." His breath feathered across her ear lobe. "You have to remember I'm in charge. You don't choose when and where you find pleasure. I do. But then, I have a feeling you need a little breaking in. Knew you would be a spirited sub." He paused, then said, "Remember, you have a safe word—if you're ready to quit."

She frowned, irritation slinking down her spine. She knew that tone. Evan was good at getting people to do what he wanted, knew what buttons to push. And even understanding he was goading her, she clenched her jaw and endured.

Another chuckle escaped and he moved away from her. He trailed his fingers down her spine, then palmed her still-tingling ass.

"You play a good game, May, but I think I need to take this up a notch."

He moved away from her then, and again, he made little noise. She was sure in normal situations she wouldn't have heard him, but now, she sensed him. Something in her had connected to him. Anticipation soared again, and she had a feeling Evan was pacing himself...another effort to control her. In most cases, she'd have been pissed. May liked to control every situation—but apparently not this one. Now her body warmed, waited, eagerness dancing along her nerve endings. With each minute that ticked by, her arousal heightened. Not being able to see what was going on had her mind racing, her body humming. At the moment she thought she could not wait any longer, he moved back to her.

"The one thing you will have to learn is who is in charge, who calls the shots. I'm not sure you completely believe that you shouldn't be the one in control."

He slipped his hand between her legs, his fingers tracing over her soaked folds. She bit her lip again. Evan must have sensed it because he thrust a finger into her. This time she could not stop the moan. He pulled almost all the way out, then shoved it back in.

Each little thrust pushed her further to the pinnacle. Tension gathered in the pit of her stomach, tightened. She could feel her orgasm coming, feel her body tensing, preparing.

Then...he stopped. He leaned over her, his chest against her back. She could feel his heart beat as out of control as hers. She could feel his jean-encased cock hard against her rear. His breath feathered over her ear as he leaned even closer. "Don't think you can control anything. Not what is done to you, not how you feel. It is all for me to give."

His voice was low, guttural, his arousal easy to hear. He slipped his finger out of her pussy, slipping it between her cheeks. She tensed as he neared her anus, but he easily moved up her back.

"You will learn at some point that you have no control here. Every pleasure you feel is mine to give."

His hand moved away, then connected with her rear end in a hard, flat-handed slap. It jolted her, sending a rush of tingles across her flesh. She sensed him kneeling the moment before his lips made contact with cheeks. A ripple of pleasure rushed through her as he moved his mouth over her, his tongue darting out between the playful nips. A moan slipped from her lips before she could stop it.

"Ah, good girl." He nipped the fullest part of her right cheek. He continued moving his mouth over her cheeks as his hand slipped between her legs. "Damn, woman, you're soaking my hand."

May could feel her face turning red, but she ignored it. She knew she was wet. She was damn near close to losing it. And dammit, he was moving his hand over her mound, teasing her, skimming over her clit. Everything was tensed. Her body was poised for release once again but it was just out of reach. Up and over, again and again, touching, but barely any pressure, not enough to get her to come. The fourth time, she growled.

He chuckled. "Frustrated?"

She didn't answer at first, and his hand stilled. Seconds

ticked and her body demanded completion.

"Yes."

His hand started to move again."Hmm. Good. Just remember, don't come unless I say so."

She wanted to blast him, but at this moment, she couldn't. She needed to come, needed that release, and at the moment, she would do anything to achieve it. Tears streamed down her face as a maelstrom of emotion swept through her. Shame and arousal shifted through her. At that point, he increased the pressure with his hand, pressing hard against her clit. Her orgasm shimmered in the distance, right there for her to take, but she hesitated, waited, and he must of have felt it. Felt her need to hear his order.

He pressed again and she had to curl her toes into the floor and order her body to hold on. She needed it, needed to feel the pleasant rush of release. But she could hold back, needed to because she now needed Evan to give her permission.

He moved slipped a finger between her folds, his thrusts demanding.

"Yes, baby, that's it. Come for me."

For a split second, she couldn't respond, her body froze at the order. Every emotion she had been trying to fight seemed to crash through her, sending her brain function into disarray.

"Dammit, May. Do it now." The harsh, guttural demand sent her soaring, her whole body convulsing with her orgasm. He didn't stop there, but kept pushing her, driving his finger into her. As her body started to come down from her release, he pushed her up and over a second time. This time, she screamed, her body shivering from the release as it rolled through her.

Moments later, his hands moved over her slick flesh, up her body to her wrists. He released the cuffs and pulled her up and into his arms. The next thing she knew he was laying her on something that felt like a bed. He brushed the backs of his fingers over her cheek, and she thought he would take off her blindfold. But the next second, he was moving away. Before she could react, he was gone. She slipped her fingers beneath the soft fabric and pulled it off. She blinked against the lights and looked around. She was in another room, small, with a bed and little else. One glance told her no one could see her here, that she was hidden from view...and all alone.

She could not stop the feeling of abandonment that swelled. He had pushed her through submission, something so intimate, and he'd left her. As if she were no different than any other woman, which she figured to him she wasn't. Tears pressed against the backs of her eyes and she willed them way. It was just what she'd gone through, and she shouldn't expect him to feel what she did. He had given her something she had never really had before. Nothing could have prepared her for that, and she knew now it was just the start. So she would not fall apart because he disappeared.

The door opened and May's heart jumped in excitement, only to have it plummet when she recognized the sub who had led her to the room earlier. The smile she offered May was one of understanding.

"Micah thought you might need this."

May looked at the thick, soft black robe the woman held out to her. Without a word, she stood and almost collapsed back down on the bed. With determination, she steadied herself and took the robe.

"Your clothes are in the closet."

May nodded silently as the door shut behind the sub. For a moment, the wonderful tingle her orgasm had given her seemed to fade, the enjoyment turning to numbness. She pulled on the robe, her mind unable to form a thought. When she saw Cynthia's head pop in, she couldn't stop the disappointment from crashing in on her. Before she could stop them, tears welled up in her eyes.

"Oh, honey." Cynthia rushed forward as the door shut behind her. She sat next to May on the bed and slipped an arm over her shoulders. "It's okay."

She turned her head into her friend's shoulder and allowed all the emotions she'd felt bubble up and take her over. It only took a minute or two for May to bring herself back in control. She pulled away from Cynthia.

"I'm sorry."

Cynthia shook her head. "No. Don't be. While it is liberating, it can be emotionally draining."

"I thought..."

"What, honey? What did you think?"

That Evan would be here comforting her. But she didn't want to say that out loud and embarrass herself further. It was bad enough he'd run out on her. She could never voice her deepest need and embarrass herself. She needed him, needed his arms wrapped around her, comforting her. That would never happen.

"Would you mind waiting outside?"

"Not at all. Get dressed and meet me outside the door."

She nodded and waited until Cynthia left her. What the hell had she thought would happen? So he gave her an orgasm. So what? It had been the most powerful, knock-her-socks-off and leave-her-dying kind of orgasm, but she could handle it. Tonight had proved two things. One, she was a sub. That she knew in her heart and soul now. Secondly, Evan Chambers would never be the man for her. She wanted the man she thought Evan was, and he just didn't exist. The cold shell of a man who could give her an experience like that without it affecting him was just not for her.

Now she just had to figure out how to find a man who could make her come like there was no tomorrow. She sighed, pushed her thoughts aside and started to get dressed. She would focus on the positive. She knew she was a sub, and now all she needed was her Dom.

Chapter Nine

Evan poured three fingers of whiskey and knocked it back. When he lowered his hand, he realized it was shaking. Jesus. He was a mess. He had never had such a reaction when performing in the club. When he was on display, he never had sex, not once. That smacked too much of doing porno, and while he knew it didn't bother others, Evan had never wanted to go that far. Until tonight.

He heard the door to the office open behind him and without turning around he knew it was Micah. Evan poured himself another shot.

"I haven't seen you drink that fast in years."

Shit, he didn't need this. He wasn't in the mood for dealing with Micah, or his speculation. He knew it would end in a fight.

"Leave it."

"It wasn't that long of a performance for you to be this thirsty."

Slowly, he turned around. "I'm not in the mood, Micah."

His friend cocked his head and studied him. "Apparently not."

Evan tossed back the shot and set it down with a click, but he said nothing else.

"You rushed through that like you couldn't control it."

"You're critiquing my performance?"

"I've seen you work a sub over for much longer. This was...well, faster than everyone expected."

He said nothing, didn't so much as flinch. He refused to explain it. How could he? In all the years he had been a Dom, he had never had a sub get to him. She had been completely under his power. But from the moment he'd touched May, he had barely held onto his own control. Even now, his body vibrated, and he figured he could hammer a ten-inch spike into the ground with his cock.

"No comment?"

"I said to leave it. Now I'm going back down there—"

"She's already gone."

"What the hell do you mean?"

"Jesus, Chambers, you left her down there after you made her publicly submit for her first time."

"I didn't come up with the damned idea."

"But you know how vulnerable she was at that point and you left her alone down there. After cleaning up, which you should have helped with, she dressed and left. I let her out the back way."

"And you didn't think to let me know?"

He crossed his arms over his chest. "Why would I? You acted as if you didn't give a damn about her. You treated her like a whore."

"Fuck you."

"What would you call it?"

"I think you have it wrong. It wasn't about my satisfaction."

Micah opened his mouth, but Evan didn't want to hear it.

"Just let it go."

He closed his mouth and gave Evan a short, abrupt nod. Without another word, Evan left his friend and used the back stairs to leave the club. He didn't think he could handle any other questions or comments from anyone else. But he should have known better. When he stepped outside, Chris was standing by Evan's truck.

"I already went through this with Micah and I am not in the mood to deal with you."

Chris nodded. "Just wanted to make sure you're okay. Cynthia was a little worried."

Evan unlocked his door. "There is no reason to worry."

"Evan." Chris waited until he looked at him. "I love you like a brother, you know that. I just wanted to remind you I'm just a phone call away."

Lights shone in the parking lot as Cynthia's car drove up. She rolled down the window and smiled at him. "Hey, Evan. You ready, babe?"

Chris nodded and headed toward the car. Evan felt the familiar envy twist in his gut. But he couldn't let Chris go like this. Micah wouldn't worry about Evan, but Chris would.

"I'll call if I need you."

Chris raised his hand over his head and Cynthia smiled at him as she shifted the car into drive and headed out of the parking lot. Evan slid into the cab of his pickup, slammed the door and started the engine. He knew that Chris would happily snuggle up to Cynthia and never think about another woman, never need one. Evan had never thought he wanted that, but he did now. But with his background, his tainted blood...he just couldn't risk it. Didn't want to.

Wishing for things he could not have, would never have, was a waste of time and energy. He had come to terms with it years ago and he would deal with it, but not tonight.

May rolled over and winced at the bright light streaming through her window. She pulled up her sheets and sighed with pleasure when it offered some relief from the blazing intensity of the midmorning Hawaiian sun. She shifted her weight to settle more comfortably into the mattress.

Lord, her body felt used. Not in a bad way. But in a pleasant, thoroughly satisfying way. The experience last night with Evan went beyond anything she had ever imagined. Her sex clenched at the memory of her orgasm. No one, not one man, or even May herself, had ever made her come so hard. She'd lost her virginity at the ripe old age of eighteen, years behind most of her friends. She hadn't been a prude, or innocent for that matter. There'd been a few men, many of them clueless to what she needed, but she couldn't really blame them. She hadn't really had an inkling to what she needed until a few months ago. Last night cemented her opinion that she needed something more from her lover. Now she just had to find one that would understand.

Her door flew open, slapping against the wall. Damn, there was going to be another hole from the doorknob.

"Hey, May, you getting up anytime soon?" Her eighteen-year-old brother bellowed.

She snuggled deeper beneath the covers. "Bite me, Danny. It's my day off."

"Dad says you need to get up because the contractor is comin' over."

"And this is important to me why?"

"Dad took Granddad to his doctor's appointment."

Crap. That was supposed to be her job this morning. Pulling down the light blue sheet she squinted at him. He was leaning against the doorjamb, munching on an apple.

"Can't you take care of it?" She knew the answer even before she heard it, but she thought she'd give it a try.

"No. Dad said that you needed to deal with him because you know what he wants done."

The door bell rung, the dogs sent up the alarm, and May groaned. Damn, she was stuck dealing with the contractor.

"Let him in," she said, sitting up and stretching. "Please tell me there's some coffee."

"Yeah. Dad said you had a late night and started it before he left fifteen minutes ago."

After he left her, she slid off the mattress and headed to the bathroom. Within five minutes, she'd pulled herself together, brushed her teeth and thrown on some clothes. She might look like death warmed over, but she would handle it.

The murmur of voices reached her as she rounded the corner. She couldn't distinguish between the two men, other than one was deeper, more mature. She wasn't prepared for the sight of Evan Chambers leaning up against her kitchen counter sipping coffee.

She came to an abrupt stop in the doorway and blinked, thinking he would disappear and it was all a dream. But there he was, joking about something with Danny.

"Evan?"

He jolted at the sound of her voice, a bit of his coffee spilling out of his cup onto his T-shirt. When he turned to her, his eyes narrowed in disbelief. "May? What the hell are you doing here?"

Dying of embarrassment, that's what. Heat filled her cheeks and she knew she was blushing. Dammit, life wasn't fair. She wasn't ready for this, to see him, to deal with what had happened last night. Or the way he'd left her there. She needed time to get her armor back in place before handling the sight of him. And he had the nerve to show up looking gorgeous. Wasn't that just like a man? He looked refreshed. The blue T-shirt stretched across his well-muscled chest. The soft worn jeans hugged his hips and cupped his sex, leaving little to the imagination.

"May?"

She shook herself out of her thoughts. "Um, my house, bruddah."

"I had no idea."

Even hearing the disbelief in his voice didn't convince her.

"How many Aiona's do you know?"

Evan's eyebrows knitted together as he frowned. "It isn't like it's an uncommon name in Hawaii. And seriously, I would've put it together if you had talked to me about the renovations, but I've never met your father. Still haven't."

"You two know each other?" Danny asked. The rigidness of his posture told her he was ready to jump into the middle and demand answers. She definitely didn't need that.

She glanced at Evan. "Yeah. Evan is Chris's friend."

Evan cocked his head to one side, studying her. "I thought we were friends."

She closed her eyes and rubbed her temple. "Yeah, of a sort. I need coffee."

After pouring and doctoring her coffee, she leaned against the opposite counter from the one Evan had claimed.

"Did my father tell you what he wanted?"

Evan nodded. "Yeah. Well, sort of."

She snorted. "That's Dad for you." She took another sip and then pushed away from the counter. "I'll show you what he wants out back."

"I'll help."

She stopped and looked her brother. The suspicious slant to his eyes made her want to sigh, but she didn't. It'd make him even more defensive. "Danny, I think I can handle it."

"He's a strange man."

Irritation slipped over her but she fought back the need to smack him. He wasn't even looking at her now but was engaged in a staring showdown with Evan. God, she was getting sick of men telling her what to do. They all acted as if she were in idiot. Not in the mood for fighting egos, May stepped into his line of vision.

Settling one hand on her hip, she said, "Listen, bra. I can take care of myself. Don't you have a final today in American History?"

He blinked and looked down at her. A blush crept up his cheeks, and she realized she'd embarrassed him in front of Evan. She kept forgetting he wasn't a little boy anymore. As the youngest of the Aionas, he was just starting his adulthood, but he would always be the baby. He might have four inches on her, but she'd practically raised him. She'd be damned if he would tell her what to do.

"Um, yeah." He cleared his throat. "I'll be in my room, so call if you need me." With one last hard stare at Evan, Danny left them alone.

"Sorry about that. He's at that age where testosterone surges and he does stupid things." She turned toward the sliding glass door that led to the lanai. "But then, that describes most of the male population."

Evan chuckled, and just like always, her pulse scrambled. No matter what the situation, he always sounded like slow and easy sex when he laughed. After his abandonment last night, she should be able to control herself, but apparently that didn't matter. It should have reminded her just how he viewed women. They were interchangeable in a situation like her submission.

"No problem, May. Truthfully, I think you were a little hard on him. He's just looking out for you."

She grunted as she stepped out onto the pavement of the lanai. "I'm not used to it and I don't need it. Not this morning."

He brushed his fingers over her shoulder. Heat radiated from that spot. Her nerves jumped, as did her heart rate. She looked back over her shoulder at him and he yanked his hand back as if caught stealing cookies.

"No touching." She bit both words from behind clenched teeth.

His gaze traveled down her body, reminding her of everything that had transpired the night before. Heat licked down her spine when one corner of his mouth kicked up.

"You didn't complain last night."

Evan didn't cringe at the baleful look May gave him, but it was a close call. He'd told himself over and over he would never touch her again, never give in to the temptation. Hell, he'd sworn a solemn oath not to even mention it. But they were alone less than five minutes and he couldn't resist.

It was inevitable. That's why he'd always kept his hands to himself. But she'd turned that corner, her eyes still drowsy from sleep, and lust had slammed into him like a hard, fast fist to the jaw. He wanted to touch, to taste, to hear her scream while she came. Again.

From the evil expression on May's face, she wasn't going to put up with it.

She stepped around him and shut the door. Grabbing him by the arm, she pulled him away from the house and into the yard.

"Don't even mention that in my house."

He knew that many people lived two lives. They had to. Prejudices about the lifestyle were common and could cost some people their jobs or even lose them friends. But still, he didn't like the cold look in her eyes, or the dismissive tone in her voice. He knew it'd been a one-shot thing, but he wouldn't let her deny it.

"Are you ashamed of what you did last night?" He leaned closer, knowing he was being an ass, but he couldn't seem to stop himself. "I thought you knew what you wanted. You sure acted like it."

Again, a flush crept up her neck and then blossomed onto her face. "I know what I want in the bedroom." She jerked her shoulder. "Or at least I'm trying to figure it out. What I don't need is my teenager brother to overhear and take it the wrong way."

He knew that was true. But it didn't stop the need clawing at his belly to hear her say it mattered. That last night had changed her life as much as it had changed his. He knew a sub's first time wasn't something they ever forgot and he'd initiated more than a few through the years. But last night had been different.

The half a bottle of whiskey he'd downed the night before hadn't helped him. He'd spent almost every fucking minute since they'd parted thinking about her, wishing he'd gained more than her pleasure. Wishing he had truly become her Dom. The need to have her submit to him and only him had scared him shitless. Possessiveness wasn't a familiar feeling to Evan. And he damned sure never felt it for a sub.

"I take it my father gave you enough specifics to get out here, but not enough to know exactly what he wants?"

"Are you going to pretend that nothing happened?"

She sighed lustily and looked at him. "What happened was just an act. You weren't participating so much as causing my reaction. I know your rep around the club."

He frowned. "Well, seeing that I don't know what this rep is, why don't you tell me?"

She set her coffee down on a glass patio table, crossed her arms beneath her breasts and very nearly sneered at him. "You see your *performances* as just that. There is no connection between you and the sub you're working. I believe the quote I heard from one woman was that you had ice for blood."

That was the way Evan usually kept it, the way he preferred it. When he worked with a sub at the club, it was just that, work. It wasn't a relationship. While he did feel some connection with whomever he was working with, it ended when he walked out of the room. He wasn't like some of the Doms at the club who had relationships in real life with subs they'd worked with at Rough 'n Ready. He'd never even contemplated the idea before last night. And wasn't it just his shitty luck that had him thinking it about a woman who was too damn good for him. Still, the fact she was dismissing what had happened between them last night as routine was starting to piss him off. Irrational, yes, but he really didn't give a fuck.

"You know better than to listen to gossip."

She threw her hands up in defeat. "I'm not in the mood to discuss anything about last night."

He wasn't either, but he was perversely irritated that she didn't want to. What kind of woman was she? Evan had been pretty sure before last night. He'd been sure that at some point she'd settled down with a steady man and have boring sex. Because in his mind, May wasn't ever supposed to enjoy sex with another man. Not that he'd ever find out, or be on the receiving end, but he definitely expected her to follow the pattern. She didn't.

Hell, she'd shaken his world. He'd never broken in a sub who was so responsive. With the right Dom, she'd be unbelievable. Some nameless, faceless bastard who would have the right to touch her, pleasure her, fuck her.

"What the hell are you scowling at?"

Her question brought him out of his dark thoughts. "Nothing." He shoved his hands in pockets of his jeans to keep from reaching out to her again. He had already tested the limits of his control. "Why don't you tell me what your father wants?"

She studied him for a second or two and then blew out a breath. "He wants to expand the concrete on the lanai and cover it."

Before he could ask her the particulars, the sliding glass door opened. A rounded man who had to be her father stepped out smiling. He wore a University of Hawaii ball cap, a dark green shirt with the same emblem and tan shorts. Like May, he was barefoot.

"Ah, Maylea, you got started with Mr. Chambers."

May choked on the coffee she'd just drank. She cleared her throat. "Yeah. Evan this is my father, Daniel Aiona. Dad, Evan."

Daniel hurried over, a wide smile stretching his lips. He offered his hand. "Great to meet you in person. May talked about your company and the renovations you did at Dupree's, so I decided to give you a call."

Evan took his offered hand and shook it, amazed at the strength behind it. Her father wasn't old but he was slight in build. An inch taller than his daughter, Daniel showed signs of his age in a few weathered wrinkles around his mouth and eyes, telling Evan he smiled a lot. He released Evan's hand and then slung his arm over May's shoulders. The easiness of the

120

action told him what he'd suspected about May's family.

Daniel's genial manner would probably do a one-eighty if he knew what had transpired last night.

"I appreciate it. That job I did for Chris brought in a lot of business."

"I also asked around. You have a good reputation."

May looked at her father, over at Evan and back to her father. "Since you're here I'll let you take over."

She tried to wiggle away, but her father's grip tightened.

"No, no. I need you here. Besides, I got you a date for tonight."

Every muscle in May's body stilled. "A date?"

"Yeah, your grandfather has a new doctor, smart kid."

She pursed her lips, a sure sign she was pissed. Evan didn't blame her. What the hell did her father think he was doing setting her up on dates? With a fucking doctor. As if she would be interested in a doctor.

"I'm working tonight."

"Did I say tonight?" Her father gave her an indulgent smile. "I meant Monday."

Irritation rose off her in waves so strong, Evan was amazed her father didn't sense it. "I don't want to go out with him."

The even tone in her voice had Evan cringing inwardly. Her father just smiled. "You haven't met him. You will when you meet him."

Evan watched her jaw flex as she ground her teeth together, but amazingly, she didn't smack her father upside the head. She'd curled her fingers into the palm of her hand, telling him she had seriously thought about doing it, but she restrained herself.

"Dad—"

Her father waved her away. "Why don't you go make sure that brother of yours is actually studying?"

She opened her mouth to argue, but her father turned his back on her and started talking about his plans for the lanai. With a huff, she turned on her heel and sashayed into the house, affording Evan an eyeful of her ass as she did. Because of her agitation, her swing was a bit more exaggerated than usual. It wasn't until she closed the sliding glass door behind her that Evan realized her father was giving him detailed directions.

Turning his attention to Mr. Aiona, Evan reminded himself that May was now off limits.

Chapter Ten

Evan watched the milling crowd in Rough 'n Ready, trying to decide what the hell he was doing here. It was odd, feeling like he didn't belong in the one place he always had in the past. He'd spent more nights here than he had at his own place, but now he felt as if he were a virgin at an orgy.

"Surprised to see you here tonight," Micah said.

Evan glanced at his business partner then back out onto the floor. "I don't see why you should be."

"You've been here so little, especially on weeknights. And let's just say that after the experience with Maylea, I'd think you'd be sniffing around her."

Evan tossed back the rest of his whiskey and then asked for more. As the bartender filled his glass again, he said, "You know that was a one-time thing."

"At first, I thought it would be. But I have to admit, you two seemed...in tune, I guess is the best way to describe it.

Evan grunted. "Well, as you can see, I'm looking for a sub."

When Micah didn't respond, Evan looked at him. He had crossed his arms over his chest and had one eyebrow raised.

"What?"

"Evan. What the fuck is going on in your head?"

Good question. Evan didn't have an answer. He'd been

searching for it for several days, wondering just why the hell he couldn't sleep anymore. Instead of answering, Evan shrugged and looked out on the floor. "Just need a break from work. Took on a new assignment, a lot of late hours."

"Yeah, I heard about that. That still doesn't explain why you're here."

"Jesus, Micah, get off my fucking back. I don't need this shit."

Evan spotted a sub he'd worked over before. Six feet tall, blond hair, blue eyed, with a slim attractive body, and she liked it rough. Just what he needed tonight.

He tossed back the rest of his whiskey and slammed the glass down on the bar. He was feeling pleasantly buzzed...but not enough to numb the ache he had.

"I'm off for the night."

Micah looked over at Susan and frowned but said nothing. Evan dismissed him from his mind as he moved through the patrons in search of his prey. When he reached her, he tapped her on the shoulder. She glanced back over her shoulder and smiled. At one time, that smile had driven him crazy, stirred his blood with the anticipation of making her submit to him. This time, it left his blood cold.

"Hey, Evan." Her husky voice rose over the crowd. "How're you doing tonight?"

"Fine." He leaned in to brush his lips over his cheek and breathed in her scent. The cloying over-the-top flowery perfume was another thing he used to like. Now he just wondered if she bathed in the damn stuff.

"You have a partner tonight?" he asked. Evan knew that even if she did, she would dump him in a minute for him.

She shook her head. "Nope, just got here a few minutes

ago." She cocked her head to one side and studied him. "I didn't think I'd see you here tonight."

He bit back his irritation. Why did everyone act like he had disappeared off the face of the earth? "Well, I am. Ready for a round?"

Her smiled widened, a calculating gleam sparkling in her eyes. "With you? Always."

Without another word, he grabbed her hand and pushed his way through the crowd. Need stabbed his belly, held him by the balls. He shoved aside the voice that kept chanting this was the wrong woman and practically ran down the stairs.

"No need to rush, Evan." Her voice was slightly breathless, with a touch of irritation.

He ignored her. He didn't want to think about her, about the fact he felt like he was cheating on May. May, the woman who was on a date with a fucking doctor tonight. Letting the bastard touch her, kiss her, do things to her—

"Dammit, Evan, you're hurting my hand."

Evan stopped and looked down. It was then he realized that he'd squeezed her hand so hard he was amazed he hadn't broken it. Damn, Susan wasn't delicate, but he knew he was capable of hurting her. He immediately released her hand.

"Sorry," he mumbled.

She rubbed it and nodded as he opened the door to his room. Unlike the night May was there, the curtains closed off the room to the crowd above. He wasn't in the mood. He stepped aside to allow Susan in first but then found himself standing at the threshold. He couldn't seem to get himself over it and into the room. The idea of taking another woman here felt somehow wrong...as if he were betraying May.

He raked a hand through his hair and pushed himself into

the room. He could do this, he had to do this.

"Strip."

Susan smiled, and again, it left him cold. There was no anticipation dancing in his blood as he watched her kick off her shoes and then peel off the tight black dress, revealing nothing but pale ivory skin. He didn't even get the familiar beat of arousal in his blood whenever he saw a naked woman, not to mention the idea of touching her had bile rising in his throat.

He closed his eyes and tried to remind himself it was an act, that May had been nothing but another sub. The moment he thought of her, memories of the night together came blasting back to him, washed over him and had his dick jumping to attention. He could still hear her breathless little moans, the way her breath caught each time he spanked her—

"Evan?"

Susan's voice threw a bucket of cold water on his fantasy, not to mention his cock. He opened his eyes and looked at her. Every last inch of the woman was bare, her pussy shaved, her small, pert breasts topped off with hardened nipples. And he felt...nothing.

Panic scraped the back of his throat as he tried again to conjure up some kind of arousal, tried to order his body to respond. He loved this part, of getting his sub into position, and he knew just which buttons to push with Susan. That was before May. Before she had walked in Rough 'n Ready and turned his world upside down.

Susan approached him and reached out for him, a knowing look in her gaze. He backed away and shook his head. "No. Not tonight."

He turned and moved to the door.

"Evan!"

But he said nothing as he slipped out the door and headed to the back entrance of the club. He didn't need Micah bothering him or have to handle the strange stares of their patrons. He knew they all watched him, knew that he had taken Susan down for a session. All of them would know eventually, but he didn't want to deal with it right now.

The sultry night air washed over him as he stepped out into the parking lot and headed for his truck. What the fuck was wrong with him? He'd never failed to complete a session. Even women he didn't particularly like personally had been easy to take, to work over, then fuck. He actually liked Susan and now, shit, he couldn't get it up. He shoved his hand through his hair and noticed it was shaking. He reached his truck but not in time.

"Evan!" Micah came jogging up behind him. "What the fuck is going on?"

He said nothing as he unlocked his truck and slipped inside.

Micah reached him just before he could close the door. His hand shot out and held it.

"Leave me the fuck alone." Oh, Jesus, he sounded like a little boy. He could feel the embarrassment of his action heat up his face.

"Not until you tell me what is going on. Susan's pissed, and that is one woman I would not want pissed at me. So tell me."

Evan looked at his friend and opened his mouth to explain but not one word came out. How could he tell Micah what was wrong with him if he didn't know himself?

Micah shook his head. "Never mind. Just give me a call tomorrow."

Evan gave him a curt nod then closed his door.

Chapter Eleven

May sighed with relief when her house came into view. She'd spent the last few hours lamenting her inability to tell her father no. Dennis was a nice man, but he had as much personality as a flat wave. The moment the thought popped into her head, a niggle of guilt wormed its way into her conscience. It really hadn't been that bad. The main problem was a thoroughly unavailable man was more attractive to her.

Dennis eased his car next to the curb. May looked up at the kitchen window and found her first real smile of the evening. When she turned to face Dennis, she frowned at the Chambers' Contracting Truck parked at the curb.

"I had a really great time," Dennis said as he smiled at her.

Which was a sad statement in itself. If he thought their date was a great time, he had no idea what fun was. It really was a shame she felt no spark. He was nice, probably too nice.

He smiled at her before he got out of the car and rounded the hood to open her door. Like she said, nice.

What the hell was wrong with her? Most women would kill to be in this position. Nice guy, gorgeous, running his own practice…and she was bored. Probably because she knew in the bedroom, he would be just too damn nice.

He opened her door and took her hand to help her out.

"I was wondering if you would be interested in seeing a movie tomorrow night."

"I have to work tomorrow night. I work a lot of nights at the restaurant."

He nodded. "I didn't even think about that. When is your next night off?"

She worried her bottom lip and tried to come up with some excuse, then the problems with the boss and his sister rose to her mind.

"I am not sure what my schedule is going to be like over the next few weeks. My boss is having some family problems and might have to go back to the mainland."

"Ah." He nodded, easily accepting her half-truth. He stepped on her front porch and took both her hands into his. "I'll tell you what. I'll give you a call."

She opened her mouth to disagree, but he lightly placed his fingers over her mouth. "No. Don't come up with another excuse. I have hopes that you'll change your mind."

"You are much too nice for me."

He laughed. "I doubt that."

He leaned in slowly and moved his mouth over hers. She could taste the coffee he'd had and smell the light musky scent of his aftershave. His body heat surrounded her. And although she did respond, she felt nothing. Her heart barely kicked up a notch and her body didn't heat.

When he pulled back he gave her another sweet smile. "Goodnight, Maylea."

She drew in a deep breath and watched him walk to his car. A moment later, his taillights were fading into the distance. She felt small. No, she felt worse than that. She felt like a skank. May knew she had no reason to feel that way, but she did nonetheless. A perfectly nice man had taken her to dinner, enjoyed her company, and she had spent the entire evening counting the minutes until he left.

With a sigh, she dug into her purse and pulled out her keys, but the door opened before she could use them. She expected her father but found a thoroughly irritated Evan Chambers staring at her.

"Do you always let your dates paw you?"

No hello. No, hey, been waiting for you. An insult. Well, this was her house dammit, and she would not take it.

"I think what I let my dates do or not do is not of any business of yours."

He pushed open the screen door so fast she had to step back to avoid being hit. He closed the door behind him and before she knew what was going on, he grabbed her by her arms and pulled her up onto her toes.

Even in the weak light, she could see the anger flaming in his eyes.

"I think I have every right after what we did last week."

Before she could protest, he dipped his head and slammed his mouth against hers. Irritation had her planting her hands on his chest to shove him away. Instead, she curled her fingers into his shirt and dissolved beneath his kiss.

Evan's blood was hot, his temper hotter and his irritation with himself, with May, with the whole damn situation had him losing control. He didn't care. Right now, May's mouth was soft and wet beneath his. As he slipped his hands down her body and over that beautifully rounded ass of hers, need shimmered through him.

He slanted his mouth over hers and slipped his tongue

between her lips. Oh, God, nothing tasted as good as May. She sucked on his tongue, sending a shaft of heat straight down to his dick. His heart was beating so fast he thought it might jump out of his chest. He tore his mouth away from hers and kissed down the side of her neck. The essence of her was there, the light fragrance that reminded him of plumeria and May. She moved against him, causing his cock to jump. God, he wanted her, needed her right now, right here, on her porch...

He abruptly pulled away from her. In fact, it had been so fast that May almost lost her balance. He grabbed her arms to steady her. Slowly, she opened her eyes. Desire darkened her eyes and her hardened nipples were easy to see through her sheer dress.

Lord, what the hell was he thinking? He had spent the evening with her family, and now mauled her when she got home from her date.

"I shouldn't have done that."

It was all he could say, and he had to force every word from his lips. While he knew in his mind he had no right to her, his body didn't give a damn. He wanted her now, stripped naked and tied up in his bed.

He rubbed his hand over his face, trying to clear the image, but he could smell her scent on his fingers.

"Why?"

He stopped and stared at her for a second, trying to figure out just what the hell she was talking about. Her lips were reddened and swollen from his kissing. He could just imagine what they would look like as he eased his cock between them—

"Evan?"

He shook his head to clear the image, but his body had imprinted it on his brain. "What?"

"Why should you not have done that?"

"I shouldn't have kissed you."

"And?"

"That's it."

With a sigh, she bent to retrieve her purse and her keys. It afforded him an excellent view of her breasts.

"So you think you have nothing else to apologize for?"

"No."

"I think you do. How about your accusations?"

Oh, yeah, he'd forgotten about those. He was thankful for the dim light overhead because he felt his face heat up. "I didn't actually accuse you of anything."

Another sigh escaped, this time one filled with weariness. "Fine, you don't want to talk about it. I'm tired and I just want to go to bed."

He stepped aside to allow her access to the door. Panic rose, the unfamiliar feeling crashed down on him, almost drowning him. He couldn't figure it out until he realized there is a part of him that wanted to tell her, to let her know what seeing her with another man did to him.

"I was jealous."

She stilled, then slowly looked over at him. Her hand was still on the door, but she hadn't opened it.

"Jealous?"

"I saw you with that guy and I just couldn't take it."

May studied him for a second, saying nothing. The cool evening breeze played with the ends of her hair and he felt the weight of her thoughts.

"You are going to have to come up with something more believable than that, bruddah."

He should have known she wouldn't take his explanation at face value. "I…"

His throat closed up on him. He swallowed his panic now full blown. Would she think less of him because he was jealous, that he never wanted another man to touch her? When the fuck had he gotten so territorial about a woman?

"Yes?"

He shoved his hands into the front pockets of his jeans. "I was jealous. I…okay, your father kept going on about the guy and his practice and how well-liked he was and I couldn't stand it."

She crossed her arms beneath her breasts. "And?"

"And what?"

She let her arms fall, disappointment stamped all over her face. "Never mind."

May turned to leave and he couldn't let her. He hadn't always been honest with women, but he had been with May.

"I didn't know what to do. I went to Rough 'n Ready tonight, tried— Well, never mind what I tried, but I couldn't do it."

"I don't understand."

He let out a frustrated growl. "I don't want to play in that room now…unless it's with you."

A few beats of silence. "Feeling frustrated?"

He tossed her a nasty look but said nothing. Baring his soul to a woman, to anyone, was hard enough.

"I don't know what you want me to do about it."

Swallowing, he found his mouth suddenly dry. "I would like to pursue this."

She studied him. "Pursue what?"

"You're a hard woman, May."

Her lips twitched. "And you have no respect for wimps."

He laughed, although there was no humor in it. "I got to Rough 'n Ready, had a sub there ready for me, and I couldn't perform. I didn't want to." He closed his eyes, afraid to look at her, not knowing what she would think of him. He did not like giving up, admitting a vulnerability, especially to a woman. "I need you."

The silence stretched, the only sound was the occasional car passing by. After an eternity passed, he opened his eyes.

"You need me...as your sub?"

"I don't know how to explain it, but I do know that I need you...and you need me."

"I had a successful date, unlike you."

His green-eyed monster took over and he sneered, "I saw that kiss. There was no heat, no need. You were bored to death with the man."

She shrugged and looked away. "Why do you think I need you?"

"I can teach you. You know you want to learn about a D/s relationship, explore it."

Again she shrugged, but he sensed a shift, something in the air that told him he was right. "You want to know what it feels to be strapped down on my bed and fucked until you can't remember your name."

She shivered, but he was sure it wasn't because of the cool night breeze.

She glanced at him from the corner of her eye, then looked down at the porch. "And why do I need that with you?"

"You trust me."

She sighed. "In some things."

"What does that mean?"

She made a face. "Evan, you aren't faithful."

"I never said I was. Never claimed to be, but I will say that I haven't had as many women as people think."

"I just...I need to think about it."

"You can't give me an answer now?" He didn't know if he could wait any longer. The need to touch her, to see her come again and again battered at his control. It made him itchy from the inside out.

"Listen, I have waited for years for you to notice me, and now you want me to decide on a D/s relationship in fifteen minutes? I'm not even sure if we would work well together. I might do better with someone like Micah."

Before he knew what he was doing, he backed her up against the door, pressing his body against hers. Anger and frustration beat through his blood as a red haze filled his vision.

"You don't go anywhere near Micah."

She pursed her lips. "You speak as if you own me. You do not."

She pronounced every word distinctly.

"I do."

"Not unless I agree, and only in the bedroom." He opened his mouth to argue, but she held up her hand. "I have no problem with obeying you in the bedroom, but you do not own me outside of it. And I haven't even agreed to letting you have me in the bedroom. I need time to think about it."

He pressed his groin against hers and she shuddered. He bent his head to nibble on her ear. Her body was soft against his, and he knew if he pushed her, he could have her.

"I already own you. You just have to come to terms with it."

"I may want you, but it doesn't mean this is a good idea. I need time to think."

He looked down at her, irritated, frustrated, needing nothing more than to slip into her body and find relief.

"You remember how you felt? The way you felt when you came? You were so fucking wet."

She shivered again, her breasts moving against his chest, her hardened nipples easy to feel through their layers of fabric.

"I do want you, I have never denied that. What I need is a day. Jesus, Evan, one day."

He could tell from the look on her face that she wasn't playing games. Her breath was coming out in short little gasps, her skin was flushed, and her heart was beating a wild tattoo against his chest. He could press his advantage, take her now. If he did, she would submit to him, he felt it in his bones. But he didn't want that, not just one night. He didn't know what the hell was going on with him, but he did know it would take more than one night to work her out of his system.

"Okay. I'll give you two days. But I want your answer by 5 p.m. on Wednesday. Understand?"

She quickly nodded and he had to fight a smile. She might not want to say yes right now, but there was no doubt in his mind she would. And just who'd have thought May was such a good submissive?

He leaned in and took her mouth in a quick, hard kiss. Even the brief contact had both of them breathing heavily.

"You think about that for the next two nights."

He walked away, knowing he was damn sure he would too.

May squinted against the hot sun beating down on her as she pulled into the parking lot. It had been a rough two nights. Just as Evan had predicted, she had thought of that kiss and all the wondrous things it would lead to. She'd lain awake for hours each night, her body hot, her mind racing with the possibilities. Even reading some of her favorite erotic romances or time spent with her vibrator could not relieve the ache.

Why had she put herself through this? Oh, she had thought it would teach Evan a lesson. Smart move, Maylea. Seriously, who was she fooling? They both knew she was going to say yes, but she figured at least this way he knew she wasn't a pushover. And now she was too tired to function. For the first time in her adult life, she seriously thought about lying and calling in sick, but it would do no good. Until she agreed, she would get no relief.

With slow movements, she got out of her car and slammed the door. She was half way to the back entrance when she realized she had forgotten her purse. She cursed, did a one-eighty and trudged back to her car. After grabbing her purse, she headed back to the entrance. She found mail already delivered, a large envelope addressed to her on the back stoop. Odd, but then it was too big to fit in their box outside and sometimes they delivered mail early.

She unlocked the door, slipped through and remembered to flip the lock when she was inside. Chris was a bear about security, especially since the incident. If he were to pop in today and find the door unlocked, he would throw a fit.

Dropping her purse on the desk in the office, she grabbed a letter opener and pulled out the contents of the envelope. Pictures landed on the desk face up. Her breath clogged her throat as she recognized her front porch and the man there with her. In red marker there was a single word written across the glossy paper. *Whore.*

Chapter Twelve

Evan's heart hammered against his chest, his blood blazing through his veins as he strode into the Honolulu Police Department. He wanted to smash something, beat it to a pulp. He'd been at the Aiona house when May called her father to tell him what had happened, and he had immediately left. Her father acted as if it were no big deal, probably because May told him it wasn't one. But dammit, it was. This was the third time in less than a month she had been targeted. When he had called Chris, he could tell his friend was more shaken up than May's father. When Evan had said he would go to the police department to check on her, Chris had been relieved.

The need to punch something, to tear someone to shreds still burned in his gut. It took every bit of his control to keep himself from acting on the need to destroy. The days of using his fists were long gone. Since he'd learned to manage his anger, he had never allowed anything to push him this close to the edge. But with May being threatened, possessiveness and a need to protect held him by the balls.

He needed to keep it under control. He couldn't let this one incident send him over the edge. He had fought long and hard to control his temper, and he would be damned if he would lose it now.

He couldn't stop the impotent rage that thrummed through

him right now, and when he saw her sitting at a desk drinking coffee, he didn't slow as he marched toward her.

Everything in him, the rage, the terror, the feeling of helplessness, came rushing back to him as he neared her. He couldn't take the fear that tasted bitter on his tongue and stabbed him in the stomach. So instead of comforting her, he attacked her.

"What the hell is going on?"

Her head jerked up and her eyes widened when she saw him standing there. Her face was pale and he could tell from her expression that she was barely holding it together.

"I got a note today." Her voice was small in the noisy room and that pissed him off even more. When Evan got a hold of the person who'd scared her, he would make the bastard pay.

"I'll say." A detective had come over and it took Evan a moment to realize it was the same man from the night her car had been damaged. "Would you have a seat, Mr. Chambers. I'm glad Ms. Aiona called you."

Instead of sitting, he placed his hands on his hips and stared at her. "May didn't call me."

The mulish expression on May's face said he would pay for this later, but he ignored it. The idea that someone had done something to threaten her again made him want to tear the bastard to pieces.

"Please have a seat and I'll try to explain."

Evan dropped to the chair and waited.

"It seems that this person has taken pictures of Ms. Aiona...and you."

He shot her a glance, but she was studying her finger nails intently. He returned his attention to the detective.

"What kind of pictures?"

The detective cleared his throat. "You were kissing Ms. Aiona."

He whipped his head around. "In front of your house?"

She nodded without looking up. To keep himself from grabbing her and shaking some sense into her, he turned to the detective.

"What the fuck are you going to do about this?"

The man grimaced. "I offered to have a police detail protect Ms. Aiona—"

"As you should."

"And she refused."

Again he stared at the woman who had been driving him out of his mind. She was looking at him now and lifted her chin.

"You idiot."

"I don't need protection all the time. I did ask for someone to drive by the house several times during the day, and Chris is going to update the cameras around the perimeter."

"I don't think—"

"I didn't ask." Her voice raised so high, several people turned to look at them. She apparently noticed it too and her face flushed. "I need to use the bathroom. Excuse me."

She strode away and he turned back to the police detective who held up his hands. "Hey, don't give me a look like that. I tried to talk her into it, but she said she doesn't need it except at home, although we are going to have more drive-by patrols of Dupree's parking lot."

Evan nodded.

"I have to ask...do you have anyone who would want to harm you?"

"There are a lot of people who don't like me, but I can't think of anyone who would have known I was at May's the other night."

The detective nodded. "Okay, but if you think of someone, let me know. They didn't just take photos, they also did some art work. The colored pictures spilled out in front of him. Each one of them with a filthy name, whore, slut, bitch. His blood started to heat again just as May returned. When she saw the pictures she paled. Evan wanted to yell, but he shoved the need down and stepped in front of the pictures to shield her from them.

"Come on, May."

She nodded then looked over his shoulder. "Thank you so much, officer. Please let me know if there is anything else you need."

He followed May through the crowded hallways until they got outside. He squinted against the sun until he slipped on his sunglasses. Without a word, he took her hand and tugged her toward his truck.

"How did you end up here?"

"I was there when you called. Since your father seemed unconcerned with the fact you have a stalker, I felt I should call Chris."

"And he ordered you down here."

He stopped in front of the passenger door and released her. "No. I came because I was worried. The moment I heard someone had done this to you I wanted to find the bastard and kill him. Like it or not, I care about you."

Her mouth opened, but no words came out before she snapped it shut. He nodded.

"Yeah, might want to keep whatever you wanted to say to

yourself at the moment. I'm not responsible for my actions. I'm barely keeping myself from yelling."

He unlocked the door and helped her into the cab of his pickup. By the time he got seated and turned on the truck, she got her voice back.

"I don't know what to say."

The simple statement made him pause. Slowly he looked over at her. "Whether you say yes or no, if that night at Rough 'n Ready had not happened, I would still care about you. A little too much for my own comfort. I've been dealing with it for years...and now you can deal with it too."

May stared unseeingly out the window, her mind trying to deal with all of the things she had learned this morning. First the creepy photos and now this.

"What do you mean you've felt this way for a long time?"

He didn't say anything as he eased onto H-1 and around a pokey minivan.

"Evan?"

He glanced at her, the irritated look making her smile. The man did not like being backed into a corner, but what man did? Still, May needed to know.

"I've been attracted to you since I first met you."

She rolled her eyes. "You have not."

"Believe me, I know when I'm attracted to a woman."

"You treated me like a sister."

"Had to. Otherwise I would have had my hands all over you."

Again, he left her speechless—which was a hard thing to do. To think he'd been attracted to her all these years... It wasn't possible. Evan wasn't the sort of man who would keep his attraction at bay. He tended to live life to the fullest, which meant enjoying pleasures. He'd dated several women who worked at Dupree's.

"You never asked me out for a date. And you can't tell me it was because I worked at Dupree's. You dated enough of the women there, including skanky Lee."

His lips twitched, but he didn't take his gaze from the highway. "Skanky Lee. That about sums up her character."

"I did fire her for stealing."

Evan grunted and pulled to a stop when they reached the traffic lights that led to Hawaii Kai.

"What are we doing here? I need to get back to work."

"Chris doesn't want you back at work today. He wants you to take the day off."

She frowned and crossed her arms. "I can work. I'm not some wilting woman who can't handle this."

He growled. "Jesus, May, give it a break. No one thinks you're weak."

"I don't want anyone thinking that I'm shirking my duties, that's all."

"Chris said if you came in today he'd fire you."

Instead of heading into Hawaii Kai, he turned on a street that lead up to the few houses on the cliffs...where he lived.

Her heart hammered against her chest as he turned onto his street. Everything in her tensed, her mind whirling with the possibilities.

"W-what are we doing here?"

"*We* are going to get a few things straight."

Chapter Thirteen

Every nerve in her body shimmered in anticipation as he slid from his seat and then rounded the hood to her. He opened the door, grabbed her arm, then yanked her out. He slammed the door behind him and dragged her to his front door.

Once they stepped into the foyer, she sighed. Even with her hormones doing the mambo, she definitely could appreciate this house. May knew he had bought it in horrible condition and spent two years doing the remodel, and it showed. The hardwood floors gleamed. The soothing earthy colors exuded a male elegance she had not expected. But she didn't get the chance to appreciate the beauty. He gave her enough time to pull off her shoes then he dragged her down the hallway to what she expected was his bedroom. Her pulse doubled and her palms began to sweat. When they reached it, it wasn't what she expected and it must have shown on her face. He chuckled as he released her.

"Were you expecting a dungeon?"

She rubbed her wrist. "No...it's just so calming."

Several different shades of blue were filtered throughout the room. Earth tones were used here too, but in contrast to the living area, this room immediately relaxed her. Of course, that was if she ignored the California King bed in the middle of the room.

"I haven't agreed to anything."

He quirked an eyebrow.

She rolled her eyes. "Okay, you knew the answer was yes."

He nodded, but he said nothing and continued to stare at her. His gaze roamed over her body, licks of heat following in its path. Holy mother of God. He had yet to touch her and she could feel the rise of heat in her blood. Hell, even without checking she knew her panties were damp.

"You didn't contact me when you found those pictures."

For a moment, her mind stuttered to a halt at the change of subject. She was trying to control the need to jump his bones and he was talking about the pictures.

She shook her head. "Chris drove up right after I opened them. I called the police, then went and made my statement."

"I know what you did. What I want to know why you didn't contact me?"

She shrugged. Something rumbled in his chest that sounded like a growl and his nostrils flared.

"That is not acceptable."

"I just didn't think about calling you."

He didn't say anything for a few moments. "I should have been the first person you called."

She rolled her eyes and opened her mouth to argue with him, but he stopped her when he grabbed her chin. "Don't. Don't make excuses or tell me you just didn't think it was important."

She ground her teeth and kept silent.

"While your father seems very nonchalant about all of this, I'm not. This is stalking and from now on, you will tell me if you ever get something like this again."

Authority rang in his voice, and she could not help to react. She nodded, held mute by the intensity in his gaze.

"You knew you should have called me, first thing. That's why you weren't happy to see me at HPD."

She said nothing, because they both knew it was the truth.

"You promised me the other night you would call if anything happened. You disobeyed me. For that, you will be punished."

"That doesn't seem right."

He grabbed her chin again. While his touch was firm, he did not hurt her. She could tell from the intensity in his eyes that it was taking all of his control to keep his temper at bay.

"I didn't ask your opinion. I'm now giving you a direct order not to lie by omission. I want to know right away." She looked over his shoulder at the wall and he sighed. "You are just not going to give in."

He released her chin and took a step back.

"Strip."

The command caught her off-guard and she stood motionless.

"When I give an order, I mean it. Strip."

Everything in her tightened as she lifted her hands to zipper of her dress. Her fingers were shaking so badly, it took her a moment or two to get a good grip on it before she could pull it down. Her head was buzzing and her whole body tensed, ready. With a wiggle, she let the dress fall in a pool at her feet. She did nothing else and was rewarded with a quirk of his lips.

"You learn fast, Maylea." His voice had roughened, deepened. "Step out of it."

She stepped to the side of the fabric and fought the shiver of delight that danced through her. She normally would have

146

been self-conscious standing in only her bra and panties, but with Evan's hot stare roaming over her, she felt sexy. Just the way his gaze roamed over her made her feel like a goddess. She thanked the good Lord that for once she had chosen the right thing to wear. For some reason that morning her hands had gone to the red lace demi-bra and lace thong.

She moved to unhook her bra.

"No."

The command had her dropping her hands.

He stepped closer, so close she could feel his breath feather over her skin as he bent his head to her neck.

"You always smell so delicious, May. So many times I just wanted to start licking you at your toes and work my way up all your luscious skin."

She trembled at the hot words, at the desire threading through his voice. He skimmed a finger over the sensitive skin of her breasts.

"So delicate. If I had known you were wearing things like this under your clothes, I'm not sure I would've lasted this long."

He slipped her fingers between her breasts then down her torso to her pussy. She was already damp there. Her juices had started churning the moment he'd told her to strip. He moved his fingers over her, pressing against her slit. The silky fabric clung to the dampness as he pressed one finger between her folds.

"Ahh, you really do like this. I would have never known you were made to be a submissive in the bedroom. Dreamed...hoped...fantasized about it, but I never thought it would happen."

Need dripped from his voice, feeding her own. He slipped a

finger up over the top of her panties and over her mound.

"God, you're amazing." He moved behind her and with one hand, he easily undid her bra. It slipped off her shoulders, down her arms to the floor. A fresh wave of cool air hit her breasts. Her nipples hardened. Keeping one hand in her panties, he slid the other up to her breast. His front was against her back, his hardened cock easily felt through his jeans.

"I don't know if I have ever known a woman who was so responsive, in such a need for fucking as you."

May never cared that much for dirty talk in the bedroom. It had been a turn off for her, but then, it was always expected of her. Men usually expected her to take the lead and be naughty. This was different. When Evan said things like that, her whole body responded, begging for his touch.

He cupped the fullest part of her breast, his fingers pinching her nipple. The stroke had heat shooting through her blood. The light trace of his fingers had her going crazy, needing more, needing to feel his fingers slip into her. But he didn't give her the satisfaction. He kissed her neck as he continued his assault, his tongue moving over her flesh, his teeth nipping at her earlobe.

She moved against his hand and he immediately drew it out of her panties, then dropped his other from her breast. She moaned in irritation.

"You are not in charge. I thought you learned that the other night, but I see you need more instruction. Remember, your pleasure is for me to give to you, for me to build. You are under my command." With one last nip to her neck, he stepped away from her. "You broke your word. After today, you won't think of doing it again."

His dark promise had her heart galloping and every bit of moisture in her mouth drying up.

"Take off your panties, then go to the dresser and put your hands on the top." She didn't move at first, so he added. "Now, May, or your punishment will be worse than what I have planned."

She followed his orders exactly.

"Look at yourself. In the mirror."

It took her a moment to look up. She wasn't a woman who had always been comfortable with her body...or at least looked at herself naked. Her face was flush with embarrassment and excitement. But she didn't look below her neck.

Evan approached her, his gaze on hers in the mirror. "I want you to look, to see what I see."

He skimmed his hand down her spine, then around to her breast. He took a turgid nipple between his fingers, rolling it gently.

"Watch."

It took all of her control to order herself to look down at what he was doing. His hand was light against her skin, his nimble fingers easily teasing her.

"Your breasts are so responsive. Look how pretty that nipple is."

As she watched, he pulled his hand away, then moved to tease the other nipple. "I would love to put these in nipple clamps." He pinched the nipple on the word clamps.

Clamps? She would have never thought the idea sexy at all, but now, her whole body responded to the comment. Another gush of liquid filled her pussy and wet the tops of her thighs. Just watching him tease her nipple had her heart racing and she could not look away. Every stroke shot straight to her cunt.

Before she was ready for him to stop, he pulled away.

"Now, I want you to keep watching." When she closed her

eyes to gather her senses, he gave her rear end a hard, quick slap. "Obey me now, or, as I promised you, punishment will be worse, much worse."

He waited until she opened her eyes. "You will watch me...watch what I do to you."

"Yes, Sir."

Her immediate answer earned her a soft caress where he had slapped her.

He moved away and opened up a drawer. He pulled out what looked like a riding crop. "I bought this yesterday. I've been dying to use it on you since I touched it."

Her eyes widened at that statement and he nodded.

"I just knew what I wanted to do to you when I had you here, and I bought even more toys for you. But I'll not let you have them unless you learn your lesson."

He dropped his gaze from hers and concentrated on her ass. He rubbed his hand over it, squeezing it much as he had the night at the club. He slipped his fingers between her cheeks and she instantly tensed.

"You've never done anal?"

"No."

"We're going to try it."

She frowned.

"Not tonight, but we will. I want you that way. I want to slip inside that tight ass and fuck you. I can't believe with your pleasure with spanking that you haven't thought about it."

If her face got any hotter, it would go up in flames.

"Ah, you have thought about it. I figured you would have."

Of course she had. Since she'd first read it in an erotic romance, the forbidden idea had become her fantasy. To be taken so completely, in every way possible, had been a secret dream of hers for the past couple of years.

"I'll wait, though it will be hard. You need to be prepared for that." He trailed his fingers over her bottom one last time. "Spread your legs."

She did, but apparently it wasn't enough to satisfy him. He slipped the riding crop between her legs, skimming it against one thigh, then he wiggled it. It brushed against her slit, pulling another moan from her. She moved her legs so far apart she had to balance herself on the dresser.

"Good girl."

Without any other comment, he drew back his arm and swatted her bottom with the crop—hard. The sting of it against her flesh was familiar, but somehow different. He hit her rear again and again, never really hitting the same spot. As before, she loved it. The slight pain gave way to a delicious heat that crawled through her, over her skin. Heat flared out, moved through blood. The sharp sting of the crop had her gasping several times, but Evan paid no heed. He kept slapping her until she could feel her bottom had been covered. Her skin tingled, burned. With each spank, her clit throbbed. Watching him in the mirror was another aphrodisiac altogether. This was different than the night at the club. That had been about experiencing submission for the first time. Yes, Evan had been the Dom, but he hadn't been *her* Dom. He had been playing a part. This time, he wasn't. This time she would experience it completely with Evan.

He was breathing heavily when he finished, and he smoothed his hand over her rear.

"Gorgeous."

The sound of awe in his voice, the look of admiration on his face, did more than arouse her. Shame dissolved as a feeling of rightness replaced it.

"God, just seeing it all red makes me want to come right now." He leaned over and kissed her shoulder. "You like it, doncha, baby?"

"Yes."

She continued to watch him until he dipped his head and moved out of view. The moment his mouth moved over her burning flesh, she moaned. She couldn't hold that back, couldn't even begin to contemplate how to do it. The coolness of his tongue flicking over her hot skin caused her legs to quiver. She was dripping with arousal. He stopped before she was ready and he pulled away abruptly.

He caught her gaze in the mirror again, the harsh lines of his face telling her that she wasn't the only one suffering. "Come with me."

He led her to the bed and settled on top of the mattress as he pulled her between his legs.

Her nerves were overwrought. She rarely stood in front of a man naked, let alone with a light on and he being completely dressed. She stared hard at the seascape he had hung above his bed.

"Look at me."

She hesitated for the barest second.

"Do it now."

Her heart hammered at the way he shot out the command. She obeyed and watched him as he leaned forward to take a nipple in his mouth. He watched her, never breaking eye contact as his tongue slipped over one tip then the other before he wrapped his lips around one. He sucked hard, the motion shooting an arrow of heat straight to her pussy. He lifted a hand to her other breast, pinching, teasing the nipple again.

She started to close her eyes and he stopped. She looked down at him.

"I didn't say to close your eyes. You watch what I do to you."

She couldn't look away now if she wanted to. His eyes had turned darker, desire easy to see. The idea that she caused that mesmerized her.

His lips quirked as he leaned toward her breasts again, first blowing on the nipple then taking it into his mouth. She wanted to raise her hands, slip them through his silken strands, feel them slide through her fingers, but she resisted it. Evan had not allowed it. Heat flared in his eyes as he hungrily took her nipple into his mouth. He continued to watch her and she felt herself melting.

By the time he drew back, her heart hammered against her breast so hard she was sure he could hear it. The smug smile on his face made her suspect he did.

"You have the makings of a good little sub."

She didn't like his tone then, so condescending, so knowing. He must of have seen some of the thoughts on her face because he chuckled.

"If looks could kill..."

She opened her mouth, even though she knew she shouldn't. Whatever she wanted to say was lost when his hand moved to ass and gave her a quick, hard slap. The flesh was still hot from the spanking he'd given her.

"Don't think about it. I didn't ask you a question."

She rolled her lips into her mouth, pulling another chuckle out of him.

"Lord, you're a delight, May." His gaze dropped from her face, past her breasts down to her pussy. "Especially here."

His hand moved down the same path as he teased the folds of her sex again. "Jesus, you're so wet. You shaved yourself?"

She nodded.

"From now on, that's my job. I own it. I have a feeling sliding into that tight little pussy is going to be one of the best experiences of my life."

As he talked, he continued to touch her, tease her, drive her insane. The heat in his gaze had her legs trembling.

He patted the bed next to him. "Sit."

She hesitated, thinking that sounded a little too much like a dog command, but he lifted on eyebrow and she did as he obeyed. He rose and pulled off his T-shirt. She had seen him very few times without his shirt. God, he was gorgeous. He loved the sun, loved to be outdoors, and you could tell from the light brown sheen to his skin. Lordy, he had one of the most defined chests she had ever seen. She so badly wanted to skim her hands over his chest, feel the muscle move beneath his flesh. She curled her fingers into his comforter.

"May."

She didn't respond. She was too busy trying to resist leaning forward to skim her hands over his skin,

"May. Look at me." His words finally registered, but it took her awhile to raise her gaze to his. There was a hint of amusement beneath the dominant mask he wore. "I'll make you pay for that if you can't obey. Do you understand?"

"Yes."

In the next instant, he was on his knees in front of her, his gaze fastened on her pussy. Without a word, he placed a hand on each of her thighs and spread them apart. She felt so exposed, so vulnerable but she resisted pulling her legs together in embarrassment. She wasn't a virgin but this was more intimate than she had expected.

"Scoot forward."

She followed his command until her rump sat on the very edge of the mattress. As he leaned closer his breath warmed her core, drawing another gush of liquid into her sex. The pungent scent of her arousal filled the air.

"God, that's pretty. Those pretty pink lips are glistening." He touched her slit with the tip of his tongue, sliding it up over her soaked folds, teasing her clit before drawing away.

"Jesus, the taste of you is amazing." His words rushed out of him like he couldn't hold them back. The cool touch of his tongue, the amazing heat of his breath, the graze of his teeth against her clit...

Heated tension moved into her stomach, circled, clenched, shimmered close to an orgasm. But just as she neared the top, poised to freefall into pleasure, Evan pulled away.

"Dammit."

"Uh, uh, uh." He pressed his finger against her lips. "Don't speak unless spoken to. You know that."

He gained his feet, bringing his groin eyelevel. She licked her lips in anticipation but sighed when he stepped back.

"Like I said our first night, you don't control anything."

"But—"

"No buts. In this room, I control everything."

She said nothing, could not even think of something to say. Her mind had gone blank while her body lit up like the Fourth of July. He grabbed her chin and tilted her head back.

"Do you understand?"

"Yes."

His fingers tightened on her chin when she didn't

immediately answer him.

"Yes, Sir."

He stepped away, releasing her chin. His hands went to the button on his jeans. The metallic slide of his zipper filled the air. He dropped his pants, and within a few moments, he was gloriously naked. Mr. Evan Chambers didn't believe in underwear.

His erection was full, curved up against his belly.

"On your knees."

She didn't even think this time, and scrambled to her knees in front of him.

"Good girl." He stepped closer, tapped his cock against her mouth. "Open up."

She complied, and he slipped the full head of his penis past her lips. Inch by inch, he slid farther inside. The salty taste of his precome sent another shaft of heat running through her blood. She had never been one for oral sex, never liked to do more than was necessary. But now, the thought of feeling his come in her mouth, the warm liquid sliding down her throat, had her moaning around his cock.

"Yeah, that's it. Suck harder."

The head of his penis bumped against the back of her throat and her jaw started to quake from holding it open so wide, but she didn't care. His fingers clawed through her hair, twisting the strands around his hands. His frenzied moves told her he was losing control and she doubled her efforts to pull his orgasm from him. Just when she thought he was on the edge, he pulled out of her mouth with a pop.

"On the bed. Now. On your back, hands above your head. Spread those legs."

Again, she scrambled to fulfill his order, her only thought

to please him. It contradicted everything she thought she knew, but right now, she didn't care. She wanted him on top of her, in her, fucking her out of her mind. Once she did as he ordered, he moved to the right side of the bed and pulled a black strap with two cuffs attached to it from beneath the sheet. It was then that she realized the strap was across the top of the bed, and then tucked under the mattress.

He said nothing as he attached the cuffs first to one hand, then the other. "Too tight?"

"No."

He nodded and moved back to the foot of the bed. He pulled another strap from beneath the mattress and then did the same on the other side. Panic welled up as she realized he was going to have her spread eagle on his bed, unable to even move. Before she could react, he grabbed her foot and attached first one, then the other. Her heartbeat sped up a notch as the implications came crashing home.

He looked up at her. "Yes. I see you realize what this is about. You won't be able to move and every bit of the pleasure you feel you will get from me."

"Evan."

"Nothing. I want no sound unless you truly want me to stop. Not one damn sound."

He got on his knees in between her legs, his hand pumping his cock. He slipped his other hand over her mound, teasing her clit. The tiny bundle of nerves tightened with each stroke. Energy sizzled over her flesh as the pressure increased. Just as she was about to come, he pulled his hand away.

"Naughty May. I didn't give you permission."

She growled, which just caused him to chuckle as he slipped off the mattress, approached his nightstand and drew a condom out of the drawer. He quickly donned it and then joined her back on the bed.

"I know I keep stressing this, but the truth is, you haven't learned. I did not give you permission. You are not allowed to come."

He lay on top of her, his cock resting against her pussy. He flexed his hips and moaned.

"Jesus, you're wet."

He was right, she couldn't deny it. Just the idea of being tied up usually got her hot, but now, she shivered. Every nerve ending in her body danced.

He took her mouth in a bruising, possessive kiss, his tongue thrusting inside. Aggravation mixed with desire. She badly wanted to run her fingers through his hair, feel his flesh beneath her palms, but she could not do anything with her hands tethered.

He pulled away far enough to position his cock at her entrance. The need to lift her rear end off the bed, to feel him thrust home had her barely containing a scream. But instead of giving that to her, Evan skimmed the head of his cock against her slit. He smiled down at her.

"Anticipation makes it so much better."

She thrashed her head back and forth, the teasing strokes pushing her closer, but not close enough. She needed this, needed it more than she needed anything in her life. She couldn't care less about anything else. All she cared about, all she needed, was this release. When she thought she couldn't stand it anymore, Evan drew back and thrust into her.

For a moment, everything seemed to pause. Then he balanced his weight on his hands and started to move. Slowly at first, so shallow she wanted to scream. But soon, he sped up, his thrusts deep. Pressure built between her legs each time he pushed inside of her.

"May."

She couldn't respond. Everything in her was telling her to let go, to fall into pleasure, but she used every bit of her control to keep it from happening.

"May." He bent down and kissed her, slipping his tongue between her lips to gain her attention. "Come for me, baby."

The command did its job, thrusting her into a morass of ecstasy. She shuddered violently as waves of delight shimmered over her, through her. Evan continued to pump in and out of her, his thrusts now frenzied. Just as she recovered from her orgasm, she was pushed into another one, this one more intense than the first. This time, Evan joined her, shouting her name as he came.

He collapsed on her a moment later, their heavy breathing the only sounds in the room. With what seemed like super-human effort, Evan pulled himself up and then moved off her. He undid her wrists and ankles, rubbing and kissing the tender skin. Then he crawled back into bed. To her. He tugged the sheets over them and pulled her into his arms.

"Sleep, baby."

Too tired to argue, too emotionally and physically drained, she did as he commanded.

Chapter Fourteen

Evan watched May sleep snuggled up to his chest. His heart turned over. Jesus. No matter how many times he told himself it was real, he couldn't believe it.

Maylea Aiona in his bed.

He brushed the backs of his fingers over her cheek, pushing aside a lock of her silky ebony hair. He should have known it would be like this. That night at the club should have warned him what it would be like. Even with no completion, it had been intense. Now that he had…

God, he had never had a connection with a sub this way. Never. Not even the first time he had taken a sub, which was something every Dom remembered forever. After today, there would be no comparison. From the start, they connected. He knew just how far to push her, knew what buttons to push. She stirred against him, her hand moving over his chest, her palm over his heart—which turned over one more time.

He knew it would be like this. That is why he had avoided her for so long. Lord knew her submissiveness surprised him, and if he had known about it, Evan was pretty sure he wouldn't have lasted as long.

It wouldn't last. He wasn't the type of man who settled down, and he knew that more than once May had talked of kids. That wasn't an option for him—never would be. His type of background just didn't allow for it.

He felt like a bastard, but he was man enough to admit that he was starting something with her knowing there was no future. He hadn't promised her forever, but most women expected at least a little bit of a future with a guy. He knew that from their first night together. As with Doms, subs never really forgot their first time. He knew that every time she submitted she would think of him...and he had used that.

She shifted again, her leg sliding alongside his thigh. His cock twitched. Damn, the woman was asleep and all she had to do was touch him and he was ready to go at it again. Who the hell was he kidding? All she had to do was breathe and he wanted her.

"I'm getting hungry."

Of all the things he expected her to say, that had not been on the list.

"Really?"

She lifted her head. "Yeah. Is it permissible for a sub to ask for nourishment?"

He smiled. "It is."

She sat up, allowing the sheet to fall to her waist. "Well, hop to it, Chambers."

Easily, he jackknifed up, and had her on her back beneath him. He pulled her arms up above her head, held them steady with one hand. He looked down at her and his breath backed up in his lungs. Her dark hair lay in disarray over his blue sheets as she smiled up at him. Joy and arousal darkened her eyes.

"I think that you need to be taught a lesson."

She frowned as if pondering the comment. "Really? You think that I'm not quite the proper sub?"

Teasing wasn't something he regularly did in bed outside of driving a sub insane. Probably because he rarely had the woman stay over...and he admitted he didn't truly know many of them. Even while it amused him, it didn't mean the Dom in him would allow such insolence.

He raised one eyebrow. "You think you can order me to get you food? That is not acceptable."

With a saucy smirk, she asked, "Whatcha going to do about, Chambers?"

He waited a couple of seconds, then moved as quickly as possible. He had her on her stomach, her wrists anchored by his hand against the small of her back in a matter of seconds. She giggled and then moaned the moment he skated his finger down her spine.

"I think you didn't learn your lesson well enough. Put your hands out to the sides.' He released them and waited for her to obey him. "Don't move."

He left her to get another toy he'd bought her. He moved back to the bed and placed the toys on the nightstand. Her eyes widened the minute they clapped onto the anal plug and lube.

Evan smiled down at her and gently brushed the hair away from her face. "You trust me, yes?"

She looked up at him, a mixture of fear and arousal in her gaze. She licked her lips. "Yes."

He felt something shift inside of him, something that he hadn't felt in years, if ever. Grabbing the plug and lube, he joined her back on the bed. He opened the lubricant, and wet his finger. Evan was amazed to see his hand was shaking as he lowered it do her puckered hole.

"Relax, baby."

She let go of a breath and he slipped his finger inside. Her muscles clung to him and he closed his eyes. Damn, it was going to kill him to wait, but he knew had to. Her ass was so tight he would hurt her if he tried to fuck her now.

After a few minutes of stroking, May was moving with him, her hands now clutching at the sheets. He pulled his finger out and lubed up the beginner plug. Skimming his free hand over her ass cheeks to sooth her, he pushed the plug into her, past the tight ring of muscles. When he was sure it was secure, he slipping his hand under her, teasing her clit. She was already wet, her juices wetting his fingers, her clit hard and throbbing. He wanted to have some control, to draw out the pleasure, but the thought of pushing into her tight core—tighter now thanks to the plug—had him barely able to think straight.

Fast as he could, he had a condom on and was back on the bed. He pulled her up to her knees.

With more control than he actually felt, he slowly entered her, sighing over the tight feel of her pussy as it clasped down on his cock. Damn, she'd been snug before, but now he knew it was a struggle for her to take him. She pushed back against him, trying to rush him.

"No, May."

She stilled and he could hear her breathing coming out in harsh, angry huffs. It took some doing, but he worked his way into her completely. He was surrounded by her warmth, felt the occasional tug of her muscles, and he wanted nothing but to come right then. But he needed her pleasure first.

He started to slowly build her up, spanking her ass with each easy stroke. He knew her flesh was still sensitive and the plug in her ass added another level of pleasure/pain for her.

He stilled when he felt her shaking, felt her so close to coming.

"You don't come unless I tell you."

She groaned, and he slapped her ass in retaliation. Her quick intake of breath was filled with so much arousal that he shivered. Damn, there was never going to be another sub for him like May.

He dug his fingers into her skin as he started to move in earnest. The sound of her harsh breathing, the slapping of flesh against flesh, heightened his own arousal, pushed him closer to the edge. He slipped his fingers to her clit, brushed over it lightly. Not hard enough to make her come, but enough to drive her out of her mind. Soon though, the game of teasing her, of keeping her at the edge wasn't enough. He wanted to feel those muscles tighten on his cock, hear her moan in pleasure.

"Now, May."

She whimpered, pushing back against him, the movement telling him of her frustration. He continued thrusting, but her frustrated growl told him she was unable to break free. He twisted the anal plug, throwing her into her orgasm. Her body convulsed with it, pulling him deeper into her core. His balls drew up and he could no longer hold back. His own movements became uncontrolled as he pumped into her, loving the tight feel of her cunt, the way her muscles clung to him each time he pulled out. One last thrust and he came, his orgasm crashing through him, washing over him.

They both collapsed on the bed. He rolled to his side and pulled her up against him.

"Are you okay?" he asked.

"Hmmm, wonderful."

The easy pleasure he heard in her voice warmed him. He brushed her hair away from her face and placed a soft kiss on her temple. Soon, he heard her breathing even. Without another thought, he followed her into a dreamless sleep.

Sometime later, May woke, but kept her eyes closed. Her muscles were tired but completely loose. She opened her eyes then shut them. A contented smile curved her lips as she snuggled beneath the comforter. She was in Evan's room and not only that, she had agreed to become his sub. Nothing in her life would ever be able to come close to what she'd experienced. Glancing around the room, she looked for her clothes.

"I put them up."

She looked over to the doorway to find Evan standing there, his shoulder leaning against the doorjamb. Every nerve in her body tingled and her heart jumped up into her throat. He wore nothing but a pair of jeans, unbuttoned. Why did it seem that every drop of moisture in her mouth had evaporated? Oh, right. There was six foot plus of stud standing in the doorway.

She licked her lips and then froze when his gaze narrowed in on her mouth. "W-what did you say?"

It seemed to take him a minute, but he shook himself then raised his gaze to hers again. "I put your clothes up."

May frowned. "Where? I need to get dressed."

"I didn't give you permission."

"Excuse me?"

"I think you heard me. No clothes."

She opened her mouth, but he shook his head.

"I told you. I'm in charge. But I will allow you to wear one of my shirts, nothing else. I made lunch."

Good lord, he didn't expect her to go eat lunch without a pair of panties, did he? He approached the bed and held out his hand.

"Now, May."

His voice whipped out in command and her body responded. Heat flared low in her tummy as her nipples tightened. Hesitantly, she laid her hand in his. He helped her up out of bed and to her feet.

"Good girl."

He slipped his hand from hers and skimmed it down her spine to her rear end. He traced a line between her cheeks and she instantly tensed. He chuckled, a sound filled with such unadulterated masculine satisfaction she should have been pissed. Unfortunately, her body didn't give a damn. Her pussy clenched, new moisture coating her lips.

"Don't tell me you didn't like it, because you definitely did."

The heat in his voice, the way it deepened as he talked to her told he had liked it too. That it had excited him. She looked up at him as her face burned. She wasn't ashamed, but she hadn't expected to be so turned on by it. But she had been, and she couldn't wait to try it for real.

She licked her bottom lip and he groaned. Evan swooped in for a quick, hard kiss. By the time he pulled away, he was breathing heavily. He rested his forehead against hers.

"Okay, we have to stop or we won't make it to the table to eat."

A spark of heat flared from her tummy and coursed through her. Just the idea that she could cause him this amount of discomfort gave her pleasure. He moved away from her, opened one of his drawers and pulled out a T-shirt emblazoned with Chambers Contracting across the front. With fast hands, he had it over her head and then on her body. While it covered all her important parts, she still felt exposed with no panties on.

She glanced around, hoping to find them, but he caught her chin between his fingers. "No. I say no panties at the table. That is the way you will eat. Of course, if you refuse, you'll be eating naked."

She hesitated, thinking of just how sexy it would be to sit in front of Evan naked. Apparently, she hesitated long enough to make him think she was going to argue with him. He reached for her and placed his hands on her shoulders.

"Okay."

He smiled, and damn if the cocky grin didn't make her want to defy him. While she knew that he would never force her to do something she truly didn't want to, it was hard to take his cockiness. But after the challenges of the day, she knew she would need some kind of break. If it meant she sat on her tender rear during lunch, she would do it.

"Come on." He placed a hand on the small of her back. The gentlemanly gesture caught her unawares. It wasn't that she thought Evan wasn't a gentleman, but he had never touched her in that way before. He had always seemed to avoid touching her. While it spoke of their change in relationship, she had to remind herself it wasn't as if they were boyfriend and girlfriend. They were lovers, and only temporarily.

He led her out to a small dining area in his kitchen. The round, dark cherry table was set with sandwiches and potato salad. He hadn't asked what she wanted, he had just made it. She opened her mouth, but he slipped his hand down to her ass and squeezed.

"I know what you like."

She turned and studied him for a long moment. He was again challenging her and she didn't understand why. Oh, yeah, she knew he was establishing control, but if the things she did in the bedroom didn't prove his control over her she wasn't sure what would.

He guided her to her chair and pulled it out for her. Once she was seated, he settled in the chair next to her. She glanced around the kitchen, her love of cooking taking over the moment.

God, it figured he would have a beautiful kitchen. Dark wood cabinets, two ovens, a gas stovetop and subzero fridge were just a small part of the beauty.

"I didn't know you liked to cook."

He smiled, just a small curving of the lips and her heart started to beat faster. She had it bad.

"I do like to cook, but it is a rather new skill. Chris taught me a lot of what I know."

"I just thought, you're in Dupree's a lot for dinner..."

"Not for the food."

For a moment, she just watched him eat his potato salad. He wasn't a drinker, not a heavy one, so it wasn't the bar.

He sat back and sighed. "You're the reason I go there."

"Me?"

He threw her a darkly amused look. "Yeah, you. You didn't think I went there just because I loved to eat the same thing every night, did you?"

Her mind whirled with the knowledge that Evan had actually spent most nights at Dupree's for her. She couldn't seem to wrap her mind around the idea.

"You don't believe me? Have you ever noticed that I rarely show up on nights you aren't working?"

"And how was I to know that you weren't there the nights I didn't work? I wasn't there. Besides, you spent a lot of time there on the nights Lee worked."

The moment the words escaped she cursed herself for revealing that. The neediness in her voice, the almost whine she heard there embarrassed her more than sitting in the kitchen with no panties on.

"May."

She kept her concentration on her food as she picked at her potato salad.

"Maylea."

With some effort, she raised her gaze to his. She expected pity, but instead she saw tenderness, with a hint of amusement.

"Did you ever wonder why I dated her?"

She looked away again, pretending she had an appetite. She dug into her potato salad and shoved a huge amount into her mouth. The silence stretched and she could feel him studying her, waiting for her to look at him.

With a sigh, he reached over, plucked her off the seat, and dropped her into his lap. His pants were rough against her bottom. He slipped his arms around her waist. She clasped her hands together and stared at them. It was odd, this feeling of embarrassment she now felt around him, with him. She had been shy, sometimes tongue-tied, but never embarrassed to this degree.

"I dated Lee because she was the polar opposite to you."

She lifted her head and bumped his chin. "You don't have to lie to me."

He was quiet for a second before saying, "I'm not. I told you I was attracted to you from the start. I would have never guessed you would be a sub. And well, Lee was a distraction and I knew dating her would piss you off."

"You did it to irritate me?"

He chuckled. "I didn't realize it at the time. But I just had what you would call a revelation about it the other day."

She wanted to believe, wanted to buy into the whole idea that he found her more enticing than Lee. But she knew better, and if there was one thing May was good at was facing the truth.

"Lee is beautiful."

"Fishing for compliments?"

"I—"

He interrupted her. "Physically, Lee is beautiful, thanks to God and some really good plastic surgeons. But there is nothing inside of her. She has a cold heart. Hell, I'm not sure she even has a soul. You on the other hand are gorgeous inside and out. It might sound corny, but it's true."

She opened her mouth to say something but his heartfelt tone took her by surprise. It wasn't something she expected from him, about anything, especially women.

He reached over and slid her plate closer to his. "Now, if I know you, and I do more than you are probably comfortable with, you ate barely anything before you left this morning. Eat."

She wiggled to move off his lap, but he tightened his hold. "Nope, you sit here."

She frowned but knew better than to fight him. Her stomach growled, telling her to hurry and so she picked up the fork and took another bite.

They ate in silence. Well, mainly she ate, he watched. It was a bit disconcerting sitting there with barely any clothes on, the soft material of his jeans rubbing against her rear-end. Sensitive from his spankings, the friction was starting to drive her insane.

"Quit squirming." The knowing amusement she heard in his voice had her scowling. He knew exactly what it was doing to her.

She tried to concentrate on eating, but it was an impossible task. He kept nibbling on the sensitive skin just behind her ear. Each little scrape of his teeth against her flesh sent a thousand little shockwaves through her body. It seemed to leech every coherent thought from her brain.

"Evan."

"Hmm."

She moaned when he took her earlobe between his teeth and gave it a sharp little tug.

"I can't eat with you doing that."

His fingers danced up her spine then back down again. "Hmm?"

"Evan."

He sighed. "Okay."

He relented, relaxing back against the chair. Still, he toyed with the ends of her hair.

"So, when did you decide to pursue this?" he asked.

"I told you this morning—"

He shook his head. "No. D/s."

She picked up her fork and toyed with her potato salad again. How did she explain it? Granted, he would understand more than most people in her life, but it was still odd to say it out loud to him.

"I'm not really sure. I was having problems in bed. I couldn't get any satisfaction."

"You never came before?"

She rolled her eyes. "Of course I did."

"Maylea, don't lie to me."

"I've had orgasms before you."

He grabbed her chin and turned her head so that she had no choice but to look at him.

"Truth. And that's an order."

The flirtatious glint had dissolved into determination. This was not her friend, but her Dom. Even as irritation heated her blood, it intermingled with arousal. If any other man used that tone with her, she would cut him into tiny pieces. Evan did it and she could feel her pulse click up a beat and her nipples harden against the soft cotton shirt. His shirt.

"Not with a guy."

He eyed her warily. "Truth?"

Now he was just trying to embarrass her. She slammed her fork down on the plate with a clink then threw her hands up in the air. "Why would I lie about something like that?"

Evan released her chin and studied her for a moment. The house was so silent she could hear the kitchen wall clock ticking.

"I find that hard to believe but it makes sense."

"What does that mean?"

Instead of answering her, he asked, "You were only twelve when your mother died?"

She nodded.

"And you pretty much took over the family. I've seen the way you boss them all around."

She rolled her eyes. "I don't boss them. I keep it all together."

"And you've been doing it much longer than most people would be able to do."

She shrugged.

"And that is a lot of responsibility to take on as a twelve-year-old."

She had worked all of this out, had realized that her need for control to keep the family together is what had caused her to attract the wrong kind of man. She didn't want a man to order around.

"I can tell from your expression that you have figured it out. But what took so long?"

"It wasn't easy. I don't sleep around and well, when you don't have that many partners, it takes awhile to figure it out."

Evan nodded as he watched her pick up the sandwich and take a healthy bite. He was glad to see her finally eating. It wasn't as if May was too skinny, but he knew the past few days had been hard on her and her appetite had suffered. Her brother Danny had mentioned it. It had been so hard to leave her alone, to get out of that bed and allow her some rest, but he knew that she needed a respite—although he was already looking forward to taking her again. He could imagine setting her down on the strong cherry-wood table and taking another taste of that incredible pussy.

His cock twitched, threatening to bust his zipper. He shifted his weight, trying to ease the strain. "So, you didn't date much."

She finished chewing before answering. "I did date a lot. You've seen how my dad is, and well, working at the restaurant gives me access to a lot of men."

He damn well knew it. More than once he had seen a tourist pick her up for the night, and more than once he had tortured himself with the thought that she had gone home with the bastard. It was somewhat gratifying to know that she had apparently kept her standards high.

"When you don't have a lot of sex, it's hard to tell what the problem is. None of my friends had issues. They all loved it. Me, well, it left me cold. I thought I was frigid."

The statement pulled an unexpected chuckle out of him. "You are anything but frigid."

Never in all his years as a Dom had he experienced a sub

who responded so readily. There was a good chance if she had been any more responsive, he'd keel over from pleasure.

She avoided meeting his gaze and he hated that. When May was trying to avoid something, she didn't look him in the eye. Probably because she couldn't lie worth a damn.

"It isn't easy being so sheltered with the family, then you know young men...they don't always know what to do. So I waited. Nothing happened."

"But you did get aroused."

She sighed. "You aren't going to let this go."

"No. May, I'm not doing this to embarrass you."

She tossed him a look that told him she didn't believe him.

"I'm your Dom."

She smiled at him, the smile so full of satisfaction that his heart skipped a couple of beats.

"I know." The pleasure he heard in her voice made him smile.

"And in order for me to help you gain the most satisfaction, I have to understand your wants...needs."

"I realized that I found myself more attracted to romances with a really alpha guy. Especially erotic romances. Especially if there was some kind of dominance thing going on."

"So you got off when the woman was dominated."

She nodded. "I mentioned it to Cynthia and she let me borrow some books and hooked me up with some websites."

"And got Micah to give you that deal." He spat out every word, still pissed at his best friend's woman for doing that.

May placed one of her small hands on his chest, right over his heart. "Do you really mind? If it hadn't been for that, I would have never gotten the nerve to try, you would have never been forced into acting as my Dom, and we would have never gotten together."

Her soft, heartfelt words slipped over his flesh, into his blood stream and warmed his heart. She was right. If it hadn't been for that, if she hadn't been put out there in such a way, he would have never taken a chance.

"Now, I told you. You tell me."

That stopped him. "Tell you what?"

"How you became a Dom? I mean, your need to control must come from somewhere."

He shrugged. "I just get off from watching a sub be controlled."

She cocked her head to the side and the ends of her hair brushed along his forearm. "So it *is* just an act."

Jesus, he didn't mean for this to go this way, to veer off into things he didn't want to talk about. But she was looking at him with those Caribbean blue eyes, questioning him, and the worst of it was, he wanted to tell her. He wanted to tell her about his crackwhore mother and what she'd done to him, but he had never shared that with anyone other than Micah and Chris.

But from the irritated look on her face, not to mention the disappointment he heard in her voice, he had to come up with something.

"For me, it isn't so much needing the control as it is what I can give you by having the control."

She took another bite of potato salad and chewed it silently. "I'm still not sure I understand."

"May."

He waited until she turned to look at him, those expressive eyes filled with wariness and questions. He cupped one side of her face with his free hand. "I didn't know true pleasure until I had brought a sub to completion. It was like a whole new world opened up to me. Yes, I had satisfaction with straight vanilla sex, but until then, I didn't realize that I could give someone such pleasure."

She sighed and leaned forward to brush her lips gently against his mouth. The warmth of her breath, the soft, wet touch of her tongue stopped all rational thought. It was just that simple that she kissed him, wanted him, and he would not be able to control himself.

The simple gestured deepened, her tongue moving into his mouth to tangle with his, taste, savor. At the moment he wanted—no needed—her.

Somewhere in his rational mind a voice told him to stop, to gain control. It took several seconds for it to finally penetrate.

Abruptly, he pulled away, tearing his mouth from hers. Both of them were breathing heavy, and May wore an expression of triumph.

"Hmm, so you think to test out your Dom? See if you could make him lose control?"

The smile she offered him was filled with happiness...anticipation.

"I think you need to learn another lesson."

He lifted her off his lap and plopped her on the table, shoved the shirt up to her waist, pressed her legs apart and set to proving that he still had complete control of the situation.

Chapter Fifteen

May took another sip of ice tea and looked over the schedule for next week. She was stuck working out in the restaurant because Chris was busy on the phone. It had been that way since she had gotten there about eleven that morning. He'd been short tempered and a bit nasty, so she had stayed out of his way. She knew that something had to be going down if he was acting like this. Chris had an even temper, sometimes too even in her opinion, and he rarely snapped at her.

So here she sat, her body tired, her muscles feeling used, trying to concentrate on next week's schedule.

She had insisted that Evan take her home the night before. It wasn't as if her father would have complained, but seriously, she needed some sleep. She had a good idea that if she had not gone home, Evan would not have left her alone. When she realized that she was sitting staring off into space, with what she was sure was a goofy grin on her face, she shook herself and tried to get back to work. Unfortunately, the main reason she couldn't concentrate came walking through the door. Without pausing, he strode toward her. He really did have a sexy walk. All power and grace. Most of the time he looked as if he had nothing better to do, but now he seemed to be in a rush. Her heart started to beat hard against her chest, and even though she knew nothing would happen here, her body already reacted. The slow beat of arousal started thrumming through her blood, her nipples tightened and everything around her faded...everything but Evan. He slipped into the round booth, scooting all the way over to her side. The heat of him, the fresh scent of ocean-kissed air surrounded her.

Without a word, he cupped her face between his big hands and dove into her mouth. The kiss was like his walk—sexy, powerful—and it left her head spinning. He pulled back and smiled down at her.

"Hey."

She chuckled. "Hey, yourself."

He looked down at the schedule. "Are you working tonight?"

"This is for next week. But I am supposed to be off tonight. I'm going to offer to work though. The boss is in a mood."

He frowned. "Something up?"

She shrugged and picked up her pencil. "Not sure. He about bit my head off when he came in this morning and pretty much has kept the door shut. I have a feeling there might be problems at home."

"You don't think there is anything wrong with Cynthia?"

She shook her head. "No. He wouldn't be here right now if there was."

Evan nodded and started to toy with the ends of her hair.

"So I guess I can't convince you to come over tonight?"

"I guess that depends on the boss."

"What depends on me?"

Chris was standing in front of the table with his hands on his hips, regarding them with interest. Evan smiled at him. "May said she might be working tonight."

Chris grimaced and slid in opposite of them. "No, because I am going to have to ask a big favor of you, May."

"What?"

"I have to go back to the mainland, to Georgia. My sister's in the hospital."

"Oh, no. What happened?"

"I'm not really sure other than she was attacked at work, or after work...I can't get a decent fucking answer off of anyone. Mom is on her way, and I am going to take a flight out tomorrow night. Cynthia is trying to say she will go with me, but I am going to try and leave her here. She just opened the bakery and this will hurt if she pulls out and leaves."

"I think you're going to lose that battle. Besides, she just hired that new baker," May said.

He nodded. "But I gotta at least try. I'm going to close tonight, then come in tomorrow morning. I'll talk with the kitchen staff in the morning about it. I hate to ask you to work so many hours."

She shrugged. "I can handle it and if worse comes to worse, I can work split shifts. Simone has come a long way, and I can start to train her to be third key. I told you we needed one."

He smiled. "Never afraid to say you told me so. Well, I gotta get on the computer and start working on getting a flight into Atlanta."

He slipped out of the booth and both of them watched him go.

"That's not good. Jocelyn has been messed up for awhile."

"Top of her culinary class, named one of the ten top pastry chefs in the country Jocelyn?"

May nodded. "Started before Chris went back for that wedding. He's been worried."

He gave her a swift hard kiss. "Looks like you have tonight off. How about dinner at my place?"

"You cooking?"

He nodded.

"You're on. I should be done here about four."

"I'm going to check on Chris."

He gave her another quick kiss and then slipped out of the booth. Her whole body celebrated from the brief contact, but she knew better than to get used to it. She knew what they shared was unique, that Evan had never started a D/s relationship with anyone he knew really well, but she also knew it wouldn't last. Evan wasn't a man to tie down, and while she felt a little sad at that, she pushed the thoughts and feelings away. He was giving her all he could and for the moment that was enough.

But even she knew her own thoughts didn't ring true.

Evan shut the office door behind him and then settled in a chair in front of Chris's desk.

Without looking up, Chris asked, "I take it I don't have to ask you to keep an eye on May?"

Evan didn't say anything because he knew Chris didn't expect an answer. Truth was, he had told himself to stay away, to just maybe call her this afternoon. But he had checked in on the work being done at her house, had lunch with her father and grandfather, and couldn't seem to stay away. Being in her home, seeing all those pictures of her, he hadn't been able to resist stopping by.

"So you booking one or two seats?"

Chris grimaced again. "Two. Cynthia read me the riot act when I told her I was going alone. She said if it took too long, she'd go down to see Max and Anna."

"You have no idea of what is going on?"

Chris let loose a sigh that was filled with frustration and worry. "No. But I do know that she was having problems before this. She wouldn't say, but I did a little checking. That asshole she worked for has a thing for his chefs."

"You think she was dating him?"

"Hell, no. Jocelyn refuses to date anyone she works for. She said it can lead to problems, and she didn't want them. But I wonder now, and I wonder what he has to do with what happened."

"Police are no help?"

The muscle in Chris's cheek flexed. "I do know she was attacked, but that is all Mom would tell me. I can't get a hold of the detective in charge of the case. So I guess I'll find out when I get there."

"You need me to keep an eye on the apartment?"

"Nope. I'll call if we're there more than a week. So I take it things have changed between you and May?"

Evan just stared at him, refusing to say anything.

Chris laughed. "I knew you wouldn't be able to handle it after you did the submission."

"What the hell do you mean?"

"Jesus, Evan, I knew why you hung around here. We've been friends a long time and you didn't start haunting my doorway until I hired May. And then, you weren't around much when she wasn't working."

Evan could feel his face warm and Chris hooted. "Christ, Evan Chambers is blushing."

"Let it alone."

It took a few moments for Chris to bring himself under control.

"Ah, that felt good. Since I got the call this morning I have been a mess. There is one thing. Don't hurt her."

"What makes you think I would think of doing it?"

Chris waved away the question. "Shit, we're men, we fuck everything up. Just be careful with her. She loves you."

Uncomfortable with the idea, Evan shifted in his chair. "She doesn't know me."

Chris studied him for a long moment. "I think she does and that's what scares the hell out of you. Be gentle."

"So you aren't worried about your best friend?"

Chris nodded. "But then you never listen to me. I could have told you a long time ago that May would be good for you."

"There can be no long term, you know that."

"*You* think that. What your whore of a mother did to you, allowed to happen to you, it doesn't change anything."

"Let it go."

Chris sighed. "I'm going to have to because I just don't have the energy. I have to concentrate on getting to Atlanta and getting Jocelyn taken care of."

Three days later, May looked up from the hostess stand to see Detective Carino walk through the door. She smiled and he responded in kind.

"Are you here for a bite to eat or do you have info?"

"A little of both if you have a moment?"

He picked the best time, and she was sure he knew it. The mid-afternoon lull was worse than usual. The beautiful weather outside was keeping everyone out at the beach.

"No problem." After showing him to a table, she gathered up two iced teas and joined him while he looked over the menu.

"What do you suggest?"

"Kalua Pig Pizza. It's mo' better."

He smiled at her, his hazel eyes laughing. "It took me awhile to get used to that saying when I first got here."

"Where are you originally from?"

"Seattle. HPD did some recruiting up there and I decided I'd had enough rain to last a lifetime. I was ready for warm beaches and sunny days."

After Simone came to their table and took his order, he said, "We haven't made any more progress, I just found some interesting tidbits that I wanted to bounce off you."

She nodded.

"Well, your friend Rick was missing from the fundraiser that night, for a period of twenty minutes. It doesn't prove anything, but it is curious."

May shook her head. "I just don't see him doing it. He was pissed when we broke up, but I think he was just irritated that I did it before he got the chance to."

He studied her for a moment. "Might be that he has something to prove?"

"Maybe, but truth is, Rick is lazy. Revenge is one thing, but he cares more about his career and public image. Yes, I dumped him and that smarted. But in truth, once Chris threatened to have him arrested, he disappeared. He never stalked me."

"I would stay clear of him."

"I always do."

He laughed. "I also wanted to ask you about a Dr. Akito."

Her mind went blank for a moment, then she remembered the date from a few weeks earlier. "Ah, I only had one date with him. And I didn't know him beforehand. Why would you check him out?"

"When I talked to your brother, he mentioned him, and while it wasn't that important, I thought we should at least run a check on him. He was arrested for assault."

Her eyes widened. "Really? I would have never guessed. He seemed so...well, passive."

"The charges were dropped by his ex-girlfriend."

May shook her head. "But I didn't even date him before the first incident."

"Ah, your father told me he asked about you. That he had dined in here before."

A chill raced over her flesh. "That's weird."

"Yeah, so we're checking him out a little more closely. But you've had nothing else happen?"

She shook her head. "I would have contacted you otherwise. Truth be told, I've been on pins and needles, waiting. I hate it...the not knowing if or when it will happen again."

He reached out and patted her hands. "We'll get the bastard. You still have someone driving you back and forth to work?"

She nodded, still amazed that Kai and Danny had no objection to Evan taking her to and from work. It was if there had been some big male-bonding moment she'd missed out on. As if conjured up by her thoughts, Evan walked through the door, and she knew he was looking for her. It had been a week since they'd first made love, but she couldn't stop the secret thrill curling in her tummy as he zeroed in on her. His gaze passed over her, his smile widening, until he saw who she was sitting with.

Officer Carino turned to look at him, then back at her. "Is Evan Chambers the man who was here the night of the first incident?"

She nodded.

"You're involved?" Before she could answer he waved it away. "I expected it when you brought in those photos, but I had hoped..." He shook his head. "Well, that's a disappointment."

She blinked, then realized he was interested in her. It dawned on her then that not once since he had arrived had the detective called her Ms. Aiona, but May. What was with her karma? She went years without attracting any alphas, and now they seemed to be coming out of the woodwork.

"Detective. Is there something wrong?" Evan asked as he took the seat beside her.

"No, I just thought I'd let Ms. Aiona know we are still keeping on top of the situation."

Evan studied the detective for a moment then said, "That could have been done with a phone call."

Embarrassment had her face turning red. She looked at Evan and noticed that he hadn't taken his eyes off the detective, his face an expressionless mask. Dammit, she didn't need this. It was hard enough that she was losing sleep. Granted, it was because she spent every night at Evan's being thoroughly pleasured. But with the stress of running the restaurant by herself, being sick with worry about Chris and his sister, not to mention dealing with falling completely and absolutely in love with Evan, she had her breaking points.

"Evan, could I talk to you a moment...alone?"

His head whipped around, anger sparking in his gray blue

eyes. He didn't like her tone, but she didn't like his behavior.

Without waiting for an answer, she slipped out of her seat and smiled at the detective. "Was there anything else you needed?"

He glanced at Evan. "No. Just know you can call me night or day."

That earned him a growl from Evan. She shot him a nasty look. "Stay here or follow, but I have to do some paperwork in the office."

With that, she turned on her heel and marched back to the office. Damned if he was going to treat her like she was some kind of object he owned. She might be his sub, but she refused to allow him to rule over her life. She slammed the door after entering. Two seconds later it shot open. Evan stood in the doorway, looking larger than his six-three frame.

"Have you come to apologize?"

He looked nonplussed at that. "Apologize? What for?"

"Shut the door."

Again, he looked surprised, probably because she gave him an order. When he hesitated, she said, "I don't want anyone in the kitchen listening in."

His eyes softened a bit and he closed the door. He shoved his hands in his pockets and leaned against it.

"What do you think that was about?"

He studied her. "He was here to hit on you."

She nodded. "Partly."

Another growl rumbled low in his chest. This wasn't like Evan at all. He was an alpha through and through, but she had never seen him display such…loss of control.

"Are you going to stand there glowering at me?"

"If I feel like it."

Oh, God, he sounded pissed and not a little pouty. Evan Chambers pouty? Her world was just not making any sense today. And it shouldn't make him more attractive, but it did.

"You have to understand I don't need you lording over me all the time."

He sneered. "You didn't complain about it last night."

She sighed. "I have no problem giving you control in the bedroom. You know that. But what I refuse to do is give it to you all the time. Especially at work. What the hell do you think would have happened if you had started arguing with the detective?"

"He'd learn to stop sniffing around my woman."

A little jolt of joy filled her at the term *my woman*, but she pushed it aside. "And I would lose a lot of respect from my staff. It's hard enough running this place without Chris around to help me. Do you think I need this right now?"

"I wasn't going to cause a scene."

She didn't say anything, just crossed her arms beneath her breasts and raised an eyebrow. He rolled his eyes and moved to the chair and collapsed.

"Okay, I wasn't planning on it. But I could tell by the way he was looking at you that he wanted you."

She threw her hands up in the air. "Why would I want him when I have you?"

His lips curved. "Is that supposed to make me feel better?"

"It's the truth."

She couldn't lie, would never be someone who could hide her feelings. It would probably come back to bite her in the ass. Honest people tended to get hurt. But she just would not falsify her feelings. It wasn't the way she was made.

"Still, it doesn't mean I will put up with your bull-headed behavior. This is as bad as when you went after Rick."

"Bastard hasn't bothered you since, has he?"

The satisfaction in his voice ignited her temper. "He wasn't bothering me before. He'd stopped months ago, so I don't know what the hell you think you did." He opened his mouth to argue, but she plowed ahead. "I need you to understand that while you are in charge in the bedroom, *I* am in charge of my own life."

His smile faded, his eyes turning cold.

"Are you trying to tell me that our relationship doesn't extend outside of the bedroom?"

"Yeah, like I could stop that if I wanted to, which I don't. I care about you, Evan, but what I need from you is some understanding. I have to be in charge here, I have to be the one who handles all the fires, especially with Chris gone. If I lose my employees' respect because my lover comes barging in and punches an officer, I won't have much credibility. It would be worse than Rick showing up here."

His eyes narrowed. "What do you mean? I'm worse than that jackass?"

She sighed again and rubbed her temples. Her head was starting to pound. "No. But I wasn't involved with him by then. I'm involved with you."

His temper seemed to cool. "I'm sorry. How about I make it up with a late dinner at my place?"

She shook her head. She wanted to, wanted it more than was good for her own thoughts. For years now, she'd had these feelings for him. Now that they were involved, they were bigger, so big they scared the hell of her. She needed some space, and dammit, she needed some rest.

"No. I need to stay home tonight."

He said nothing, studying her. "Is this some kind of power play?"

"Jesus, Evan, I need a good night's sleep. I'm working split shifts and double shifts, trying to keep this place going in Chris's absence, and at night you aren't letting me get any rest. Do I look particularly well-rested?"

"You didn't say anything about it earlier."

She threw her hands up in the air. "You mean when I was rushing out the door because I was late again? I have a headache starting, my back is aching, and thank the good Lord, Simone is opening tomorrow. I will get to sleep in, then we can do something tomorrow night."

"I might be busy tomorrow."

His words lashed out at her, but this was one case she could be just as mean. "Fine. Either way, I'm staying home tonight. I'm getting some sleep." *And figuring out what the hell I've gotten myself into.* She couldn't say that out loud, but she sensed he might have picked up on it.

Without a word, he stood and walked around the table. Grabbing her arms, he pulled her out of the chair and took her mouth in a bruising, possessive kiss. The heat of it had her melting, had her whole body lighting up like fireworks at Magic Island. She speared her hands through his hair while she pressed her body against him. Every cell of her being cried out for more, wanted, needed to have him take her here, but he pulled away, releasing her so abruptly that she almost lost her balance. When she opened her eyes, she found him staring at her as if she were poison.

"Evan..."

"Call me if you change your mind."

With that, he strode out, his anger and the passion he had stirred still clinging to the air. May collapsed into her chair, her body humming and her mind numb. Her vision blurred and it took her a moment to realize she was crying. It wasn't her way, she wasn't a bawler, but she felt the need to have a good cry well up and overtake her. She was so tired, so ready to just lay her head down on the desk and fall asleep for a month. Tears poured, streaking down her face as she laid her head down on her desk. Several minutes later, she brought herself back under control. Drawing in a deep breath, cleaned up her face with a tissue, then pulled out a mirror she kept handy to clean up the damage. Her eyes were red, but not worse than they had been lately...though a little puffier. When she felt better, she grabbed a bottle of water from the office fridge and got to work on the paperwork. The sooner this was done, the sooner she could get home and sink into oblivion.

Chapter Sixteen

Evan slipped his key into the slot and unlocked the door to May's house. He didn't think he was breaking any rules, but he moved as silently as possible. Her father, Daniel, had given him the key so that he could come and go as he needed while working on the house. Granted, he probably hadn't thought that Evan would use it to let himself into May's room, but he shrugged away the guilt. He turned the corner that lead to May's room, and stopped when he saw the dogs blocking the entryway. He waited until he saw both their tails thumping in their regular greeting. He released a relieved sigh. He didn't need the damn dogs waking up everyone in the house.

It was bad enough that he was there. One night. She asked for one night and he couldn't give it to her. Worse, it wasn't so much as to have sex with her, but to feel her in bed sleeping next to him. It had been a little over a week since their first time together and he couldn't survive one night without her. Worse, he didn't have the balls to ask. Instead, he was sneaking down her hallway like a thief. Lord, if they could see him at Rough 'n Ready.

He reached her door and slowly turned the knob. As silently as he could, he slipped into her room and then shut the door behind him.

He could see her lying there, the moonlight washing over

her skin. The flutter of breeze filtered through the room and the smell of plumeria filled his senses. All his recriminations dissolved the moment he saw her there, snuggled up to the pillow, her face relaxed. As quietly as possible, he shucked off his pants and shirt, joining her in bed without any clothes. As he slid onto the cool sheets, she turned to him, as she always did. God, he didn't think he would ever get used to this, get used to how right it felt to have her head on his chest. He knew it would never last, couldn't, but he would relish every night he could feel her just like this.

His muscles relaxed, his mind drifted, until he felt her move against him. One leg slid up his, flesh against flesh.

Okay, this was not going to be as easy as he thought it would be. She was warm, and ...was that her lips he felt against his skin?

"May?" he whispered.

A giggle was his answer. He rolled her over, stretching out on top of her. Even in the darkened room he could see the mischievous glint in her eyes, the soft smile curving her lips.

"You should behave in your daddy's house."

She arched one eyebrow. "I wasn't the one sneaking in during the middle of the night. What happened to letting me rest?"

He couldn't think of a word to say. Mainly because at this moment, her whispered words, the intimacy of the moment sharing a secret struck him like a blow to the chest. The air backed up in his lungs and his mind whirled. Nothing had every felt this so very right, ever. There had never been a woman he would giggle in bed with, or one who could challenge him so much in and out of the bedroom.

"Evan?"

Damn, he was in love with her.

He couldn't say it, couldn't tie her to him that way. May didn't understand why he could never allow himself to have kids, why he would never be able to give her a happily ever after. But he could give her now, in this moment, he wanted to show the way he felt about her.

"Evan, you're scaring me. Are you all right?"

He smiled. "I'm not sure."

Before she could ask him anything else, he bent his head and touched his lips to hers. With little licks and nips, he tasted her. This was a woman who could undo him with a look. At this moment, he wanted nothing more than to dissolve into her.

He cupped her face and deepened the kiss, dipping into her mouth to get a full taste.

With soft hands, he slid her top up and over her head. Her shorts soon followed, landing on the floor somewhere off to the side.

She didn't protest, but he stopped, raising himself up to his elbows. It took her a moment to open her eyes. Passion and something else, something that was piercing his heart, mingled there.

"May?"

She said nothing for a moment, then, "Yes."

That one word was like a lifeline. It warmed his chest, his blood, and he moved down her body, brushing his mouth over her flesh. He feasted on her breasts, his tongue first circling one, then his lips pulling it into his mouth. Her legs moved restlessly against the mattress, her fingers slipping through his hair. He looked up, noticed she was biting her lower lip, and smiled. His Maylea was a vocal lover, and it had to be killing her to keep from moaning her pleasure.

He continued his path down her body, enjoying the way her

stomach quivered as he nipped and kissed it.

She laughed, the sound both charming and arousing, the moment he dipped his tongue into her belly button. The woman was a delight, one he was sure he would never get enough of. While he had always taken direct pleasure in her release, now he took what he wanted. He continued to kiss down her body, spreading her legs apart, opening her sex to him. God, her arousal fed his own. He dipped his finger into her core, happy at the way her muscles clung, aroused at how wet she was. It was amazing that with no D/s play and very little foreplay, she was so close to orgasm. He could feel her orgasm sitting there, shimmering on the edge.

He set his mouth against her pussy, enjoyed her quick intake of breath and muffled moan. The taste of her exploded across his tongue, drugged his senses. Each time he tasted her, he was amazed at just how delicious she could be. Her legs moved restlessly against his head, pounding on the mattress, and he continued to torment her. He wanted her as hot as when he controlled her every thought, her every need. And he seemed to be doing it, without the play, without the need to lord it over her. It was as if she gave to him what he needed, a sub who understood that her pleasure was his to give. He slipped his tongue between her slit again, then up and over her plump clit. He could feel her muscles quiver, feel them brace for the onslaught of her orgasm. He pulled the nub between his teeth and sucked. A moment later, she came, her body convulsing. He lifted his head and watched her, the look of wonder, the complete satisfaction that took over her body. Wanting to see it again, he pressed his fingers into her and took her clit back into his mouth. She came again, a hard jolt traveling through her body so strong he was sure he could feel it moving through his. Now was the time, he thought. He needed to be in her, to push her up and over again, and experience that supreme feeling of completion with her. He quickly moved up her body, barely stopping to lick each of her nipples. He had the head of his cock pushing against her entranced when he cursed himself. He hadn't even thought of bringing a condom.

"May?"

She barely opened her eyes.

"I don't have protection."

"Have you been tested?"

He nodded.

"Clean?"

He nodded again.

"I'm on the pill."

It was all he needed to plunge into her core. It was amazing just how hot and tight she was, the slick feel of her pussy lips gliding over his cock. They clung to him as he pulled almost all the way out and then thrust back in to the hilt. He grabbed her hips, pulling her off the bed as he rose to his knees, angling to move deeper. It took no more than three more thrusts and she was coming again. He muffled her cry of release by kissing her, thrusting his tongue into her mouth. She immediately started to suck, pull him deeper into her mouth as he plunged into her hot core.

Frenzied now, he sped up his thrusts, losing his mind to everything but completing his own orgasm. She pulled her mouth away, and looked up at him. She trailed her fingers over his cheek, then cupped it.

"Evan. I love you." She said it so tenderly he wasn't sure he'd heard her, but he saw her lips move, understood what she'd said. Her eyes were so soft, so understanding, so accepting. With those three words, he lost it. One last deep thrust and he came, losing his seed inside of her. His orgasm seemed to last forever, his body shuddering as the last of it moved through him. He collapsed on top of her, and she immediately embraced him, her arms wrapping around him. He couldn't seem to stop shivering as she brushed her lips over his temple.

"Sleep," she whispered gently.

He obeyed the command, drifting off into a deep sleep.

The smell of sex jolted Evan first. *Fuck* was the only thing he could think. The whore had brought someone home. He had hoped she wouldn't show up. What did it tell you about a woman when her nine-year-old son wanted nothing to do with her? Hell, he always prayed that some night, some john would kill her. Unfortunately, they never did. He'd slipped into the apartment and hoped to avoid her and whatever loser she'd brought home with her. They were always the same, sad men who couldn't get laid without paying for it. His mother was trash, disgusting, but they paid her.

Silently, he moved across the living-room floor, the threadbare carpet barely muffling his movements. He heard the door open, the squeak that always seem to freeze his thoughts, chill his blood. He couldn't move. The coward in him stood there, afraid to look over. Oh, God, not tonight. Not fucking tonight. He couldn't take another man's hand on him.

"You finally made it home, you bastard." The deep smoker's voice his mother had developed lately was getting worse. The twenty-eight-year-old sounded at least fifty.

He said nothing, could think of nothing to say as she approached him.

"You have a job to do."

Those few words caused terror to well up, his throat closing up as she grabbed his shirt sleeve. She dragged him and that wasn't easy. He was skinny, but she was a fucking crackwhore who rarely ate anything but junk food. Still, he could do nothing, say nothing, because the truth was, it would make it worse.

"I owe him a lot of money, so don't cause any problems."

She opened the door to her bedroom and shoved him inside, plunging him into darkness.

Evan bolted out of bed, his heart pounding against his chest, his body slick with sweat. Terror still held him by the balls.

"Evan?"

May's soft voice felt like nails against a chalkboard. Jesus, he didn't need her right now, to let her know the darkness he held at bay most days had returned to him tonight. It wasn't any worse or better than the thousands of times he'd had the dream before, but it was somehow more difficult with this woman beside him.

"It's nothing, bad dream."

She placed one of her small hands on his forearm and caressed him. Bile rose up in his throat. After having that dream, the memory of his mother still sharp on his mind, having her touch him shamed him...disgusted him.

"Are you sure you're all right? I always feel better talking about it."

"I can't remember it. Go back to sleep."

He immediately regretted his harsh tone. Her hand slipped away and she moved over to the other side of the bed. With a sigh, he shook off the dream, pushed aside the putrid memories and snuggled up to her.

"I'm sorry. It just jolted me and left me in a nasty mood."

She opened her arms to him, pulled him close and he felt the warmth of her affection surrounded him. A soft comfort filled him, relaxed his muscles and he again drifted asleep. This time the dreams stayed away.

May lay there for a long time, her arms wrapped around him, her mind drawing conclusions her heart just did not want her to make.

Chapter Seventeen

Sun peeked through the slit in the curtains as May watched Evan dress. She wasn't sure what she was going to say, but she was going to confront this head on. This wasn't the best time, in fact it was probably the worst. But she couldn't wait. She knew something was wrong. The man she loved was holding things back from her. She had told him everything in her painful past, how she had come to realize she needed to be a sub. Evan...he had held back. Worse, after that dream last night, she was sure he was hiding even more from her.

"What was that dream about last night?"

He paused in pulling on his shirt, then tugged it all the way down. He glanced at her. "I told you it was nothing."

"You said you didn't remember. I don't believe you."

He didn't look at her. "Let it alone, May."

His cold tone stabbed her heart, but she forged ahead.

"You don't tell me anything."

This time he stared at her, the gentle lover from the night before gone.

"I said to let it alone. Why is this important?"

She drew her legs up to her chest, trying to warm herself. "I'm not even talking about the dream. I'm talking about you. You barely share anything with me."

He frowned at her. "Are we going to have a you-don't-talk-to-me talk?"

His glibness hurt, but she blinked back the tears. She didn't want him to think she was a raving baby. She had a right to know about him, know about how he became a Dom. She knew that if they had not become lovers, she would not have that right. But now that they were lovers, she felt he should tell her. He was cheating her by not sharing.

"No. What I mean is you asked me to share with you, to tell you about how I realized I was a sub. You on the other hand brushed off my questions with a slick response."

"I was being truthful."

"I wish I could believe it."

He said nothing for long moments. His only reaction to her statement was his jaw muscle working, telling her he was grinding his teeth.

"I don't understand why it is so important to you."

"I give you everything. I told you last night that I loved you. But you give me nothing in return."

"Are you expecting me to tell you that I love you?"

She shook her head, sadness and anger almost choking her. "That is how pathetic I am, I don't even expect that. But I do expect something else. You hold things back from me all the time."

"Excuse me if I can't pour out my soul in between giving you orgasms."

She flinched. "Well, I guess that put me in my place."

She slipped out of bed and pulled on her robe.

"May." His voice had softened. "I don't know what you want from me."

She turned and stared at him. "I want to know if you are in

200

this for fun...or if you want more?"

Something akin to panic washed over his face. "Is this an ultimatum?"

She shook her head. "No. But I do need to know where we stand, to understand just what I should expect from you and this relationship."

"I just thought..."

Apparently, he noticed her hard look and stopped short of saying it was all about sex. He could say it was all he wanted, she knew it wasn't true.

"So, you're dumping me," he said, his voice even more remote.

"No. But I do need some time, a day or two."

She closed her eyes trying to stem the tears that threatened to spill.

"Sounds more like you're dumping me."

She shoved a hand through her hair and opened her eyes to look at him. He looked so confused and dejected that the need to comfort him almost overwhelmed her. But that would get them nowhere.

"I'm not. I promise. With the restaurant...everything else, it's been crazy."

He shrugged and looked away. She knew at that moment she was losing him, losing what little chance they had together. Even as she felt her heart tearing in two, she knew she could not help it.

"I've got to go home and shower, then be back here to work on the lanai."

She nodded. He stepped toward her, hesitated, then turned in the direction of the door. With one last fleeting look, he slipped out, shutting the door with an almost silent click. The moment it did, she released a sigh and scrubbed her hands over her face. That had been worse than she had expected. The cold reaction...that had been worse than anger. But she didn't know what else to do. After his nightmare the night before, she had lain awake, thinking, knowing that she loved him. She thought he might love her, knew that he had the capacity. Something held him back, something dark and evil. She had felt him shivering in that dream, heard his anguished cry when he'd woken up. Something had happened in his past that made him the way he was.

She dropped onto her bed and rested her head in her hands. May had thought she could live this way, being the only one in love...at least for awhile. But the way he had loved her last night, so tenderly, so passionately, she wasn't sure she could go back to brick walls. She wanted that every time they were together, the openness, the loving. It made her yearn for things she could not have, and she needed to decide if she could live this way and hope for change, or cut bait and run.

She threw herself back on the bed with a grunt. The one thing that worried her was that she wouldn't be able to let him go.

The buzzing of his doorbell jolted Evan awake, but only for a second. The bright Hawaiian sun was piercing his eyes and his stomach threatened to evacuate the alcohol he'd drunk in the last twenty-four hours. He felt his body float, his mind drift...then the jangle of keys brought him back.

"Evan?" Micah called.

"Sweet baby Jesus." It sounded as if he were using a bullhorn. Footsteps pounded down the hall, then he heard a sigh.

"What the hell happened to you?"

Still drunk off his last whiskey binge, Evan only had enough energy to voice his feelings with a finger.

"Good God, it smells in here. What've you been doing for the last day and a half?"

Fuck. Micah wouldn't let it go. If Evan didn't tell him something, his friend would keep yelling at him.

"I needed to let loose."

He sensed his friend squatting next to the bed. Micah lifted one of Evan's lids. Bright light seared his eyeball again.

"Fuck!"

Micah chuckled. "From the smell of the whiskey, and given the fact I know you too well, I'd think saying the word is as close as you're going to get to that particular activity. Damn, boy, brush your teeth and get some damned mouthwash."

"Could you please stop fucking yelling?"

Another chuckle. "Come on, Chambers, time to face the piper."

Micah wrapped his fingers around Evan's upper arm and yanked him out of bed. The world tilted, his stomach roiled, and all of the sudden he didn't need Micah's help out of bed. He ran to the bathroom, losing most of the last bout of drinking into the toilet.

After he was finished, Micah said, "I'm going to clean up this mess. You take a shower and get your ass out here."

He glared at his friend. "I don't take orders from the likes of you, Micah."

Micah frowned at him. "You know what, Chambers? You're an ass. Take a shower and be sure to brush your teeth and for God's sake, get some clothes on."

Micah slammed the bathroom door, sending a shaft of pain lancing through Evan's brain. Knowing there was no way around it, he pulled himself up off the bathroom floor and decided to do as ordered.

Ten minutes later, Evan was feeling a little steadier, if not one hundred percent, as he walked slowly down the hall. Thankfully, his friend had taken pity on him and shut all the blinds and had the kitchen lights on dim.

He shuffled over to the kitchen table where Micah had placed a glass of water and some aspirin.

"You look better," he tossed over his shoulder.

"Fuck you."

"No, thanks. You're not my type."

Irritated, Evan lapsed into silence as he sipped his water after downing the aspirin. Micah brought over toast and set it in front of him.

"Eat. I have coffee brewing."

Evan sneered. "Well, aren't you little Miss Susie Homemaker."

Micah said nothing, and Evan knew he wouldn't. Years together had taught him that Micah had a wealth of patience. That just pissed him off more.

Instead of fighting though, Evan tore off a piece of toast and chewed it. Micah silently poured two mugs of coffee and then brought them to the table. After sitting, he did nothing but blow on his coffee, take a sip and stare at Evan.

Uncomfortable with the speculation in Micah's eyes, Evan looked away.

"You going to tell me?"

"What's there to tell? I had a few drinks."

"A few drinks? Really? It looks more like a few bottles, and probably since yesterday morning. You called in sick yesterday, then didn't call today."

He gave Micah the stink eye. "I don't work for you."

Micah grunted. "If so I would have fired your ass."

"Then what the hell are you doing here?"

"Because Jerry—you remember him, right, he's the supervisor at the business you've been ignoring for a day—called me this morning. I had to drag my own ass out of bed, and away from a particularly delicious morsel of a woman, to drag your drunken butt out of bed."

"I didn't ask you."

Micah sighed. "Shut the fuck up. You might not care, but the people working for you do. They hadn't heard from you and your secretary was worried you were dead."

Evan said nothing.

"I called them to tell them you were alive—sick—but still alive. So tell me."

"I said—"

"I know what you said. It's a load of bullshit. Son, I've known you for too long. You don't drink to get drunk. You drink for enjoyment. You don't let yourself lose control."

Evan didn't want to talk about it, not with the raw feeling of abandonment still scratching his heart.

"I take it this has to do with May."

Evan looked at him, saw the sympathy in his gaze and looked away.

"What happened?"

"Nothing. She wanted more, I didn't."

"And you decided to crawl up into a bottle of whiskey to celebrate." Micah shook his head. "Not buying it."

"I had the dream while I was at her house for the night."

Micah studied him. "So?"

"So?"

Micah shrugged. "I expected you had it on a regular basis."

"I'd fought it for the last few years."

"But let me guess. Lately, it's been popping up."

Evan nodded and decided to start on the second piece of toast now that he knew his stomach wouldn't get rid of the first piece he'd eaten.

"What did May want from you?"

"She wanted to know about the dream, then the next morning she pushed. Gave me an ultimatum."

"That being, marry me or I'll dump you."

"No. She just wanted to know what was going on with me. I guess she wanted me to tell her that I love her."

"Why didn't you?"

He shot Micah a dirty look. "I don't love her."

Micah snorted and crossed his massive arms over his chest.

"Seriously? You keep telling yourself that."

"What do you mean?"

"Ever since Chris hired her, you've been smitten."

Evan frowned. "I don't get smitten."

"God, you're such an ass. You have been intrigued by her, and until you knew for sure that she was a sub, you could tell yourself she was off limits. That changed the night of her submission. You couldn't even play at the club with Susan that night, and don't tell me you just weren't in the mood. You couldn't because you needed May. She was the only one you wanted."

"I can't have her. I can't have children."

"You've been tested?"

Evan frowned. "No. What do you mean?"

"Oh, so this is the same old bullshit about tainted blood?"

"I can't escape the fact that I have my mother's blood in me."

"Yeah, and so what? So you had a lousy mother. Join the crowd. Yours sold you to pedophiles so she could make money for drugs. Get over it."

"Gee, Dr. Phil, you're such a good therapist. Your gentle understanding just overwhelms me."

"Listen, you had a fucked-up mother. Your childhood sucked, but you survived. I was left at a truck stop when I was five because my mother wanted a night out on the town. We both had sucky childhoods. But I thought you'd moved beyond that."

"I have."

Micah's eyes narrowed as he leaned closer. "Then why are you letting that bitch win?"

"What the fuck does that mean?"

"You know, the last thing I remember about my own bitch of a mother was the way she told me she needed time away from me. 'So long, kid.' That woman had no right to be a mother, but her blood, along with the blood of a fucking wife-beating bastard mingles with my own. I refuse to let her win. So she didn't want to be a mother and left me with strangers. Fuck her. I refuse to let her be that important. You need to ask yourself if your crackwhore mother is more important than May?"

"Shit."

"I know you know you love her. It is written all there on your face. She's worth it. Don't you want to fight every obstacle to have May with you? If I were you, I would."

Micah's earnest expression and his quiet, determined words started cracking through some of Evan's desolation. Everything Micah said made sense, in some strange way. Hope seeped through the depression he'd been mired in the last day. Could it be that he had a chance with May? Could they actually work at having that happily ever after?

"Ah, I see the light is coming on."

He looked up at Micah. "Thanks."

"Well, I fed you, cleaned up the mess in here. I'm leaving that disgusting bedroom to you."

"Can you do me a favor?"

"Earth to Chambers. I already did."

"No, could you follow May home tonight? Her brother had something, a date or something, and I had told him I would."

"I thought we solved this problem. You love her, she loves you. Done."

"Yeah, but I need to give her time. She asked for it, and I need to respect that."

Micah did another eye roll as he stood and walked to the door. "Take some more advice from Dr. Micah. Don't give women too much time to think. It never ends up good for either of you."

He shut the door and Evan smiled. He would give her a day or two, then he would go to her. He just had to give her that time, and then everything would work out.

Chapter Eighteen

May was locking the door behind a couple of customers when she noticed Micah striding toward the front of the restaurant. For a moment, she couldn't wrap her mind around the idea that he was there and staring at her as if there were something wrong. Then she realized he expected her to open the door. She unlocked it and opened it a crack.

"We're already closed."

He smiled. "I've been sent to follow you home."

"Sent?"

Micah rolled his eyes and slipped through the door. "Chambers made me promise to follow you home."

She shut the door and locked it. "I don't know why he would be worried."

One eyebrow rose.

She cast her eyes heavenwards. "I haven't had a problem in a few weeks. Why Evan would worry is beyond me."

She turned and headed to the office. She had to finish the receipts before going home and collapsing into bed to stare at the ceiling. Day two of her separation from Evan had taught her one thing—she needed him. She wanted him so badly beside her she couldn't sleep and was going through the motions at work. She'd been short-tempered and nasty toward everyone, including her grandfather.

She sat behind the desk, the paperwork for the day lying in front of her. This usually took her about fifteen minutes at most, but she had already been at it for twenty. With the big bad alpha staring at her while she did it, she didn't know how much longer it would take.

"Evan is in worse shape than you are."

She shot him a look. Micah laughed and held up his hands palms out. "Hey, don't be aiming those killer looks in my direction. I'm not the one who fucked it up."

"Evan didn't fuck it up."

He crossed his ankle over his knee. "Sure, he did. If not, you wouldn't be here by yourself."

She tried to concentrate on her work, but the man just kept staring at her.

She glanced up. "What?"

He smiled. "Nothing. Just trying to discern if you're a superwoman or not?"

She frowned. "What the hell do you mean by that?"

"I always thought the woman who brought Evan Chambers to his knees would be a superhero of some kind."

"I didn't bring him to his knees."

He nodded. "The man is going to have calluses on his knees before you're done with him."

"You've known him a long time?"

"Since our first lock-up in juvie."

Her eyes widened. "Juvie? Like in juvenile detention?"

His smile faded. "Yeah, but I always thought those words too clean for what it truly is."

"Did he have something happen to him there? Something

that hurt?"

He narrowed his eyes. "Nothing good comes of spending time in juvie."

"He..."

She wanted to ask Micah, knew there was a good chance that Evan had shared things with him and Chris that he would never tell her. It felt wrong though, as if she was going behind his back...which she was. Chris and Cynthia would be back tomorrow with Jocelyn in tow, but she didn't need to bother her friend with the problems they were facing now.

"What?" Micah asked.

She hesitated, then said, "He had a really bad dream the other night."

Micah nodded. "Yeah, I expected that."

"You know what happened to him."

He nodded.

"But you won't tell me?"

"I can't. I think he needs to. I'll say it's worse than you can imagine, but it made him the man he is today, in more ways than one."

"I—" She shook her head. "I really don't know what to do."

Micah studied her for a long second, then said, "Don't turn away from him. He's working through a shitload of bad memories. Being with you probably agitated them."

"Then—"

"No. I'm not saying that to discourage you. Just know that some of the things Evan dealt with as a child are beyond what most adults could handle. He lived through it, survived, but he never really dealt with it. He needs you to help him through all the emotions that are churning. If you turn away from him right now, he might never be able to overcome his issues."

"He won't let me help."

"He will, you just have to crack that hard head of his. He needs someone who will stand up for him, to him...he needs you."

His grave voice, the sincerity in his eyes caused a lump to rise in her throat. This was a man who loved Evan like a brother...could he be right?

"You're going to have to have more guts than most women I know, because the man is a mess, but if he has a chance of working through it, it's with you. In all the years I've known him, he's never let a woman close...until you."

The silence lengthened and May felt tears sting the backs of her eyes.

He scrubbed his hand over his face. "Jesus, I *do* sound like Dr. Phil."

She laughed. "Evan says that about Chris."

"Why don't you finish up what you're doing so I can follow you home?"

Less than half an hour later she was on her way to Hawaii Kai with Micah following her. She'd not expected the classic black vette, but then, she didn't know why not. Maybe because Evan always drove trucks. The streets were slick with a recent shower, but mostly empty since it was nearing two in the morning. This area wasn't a busy place for tourists. They stayed down near Waikiki and the nightclubs and hotels. Her phone vibrated on the passenger seat and she noticed Evan's number. She grabbed it and clicked it on.

"Where are you?"

"And hello to you."

"Don't be an ass, where are you?"

"I'm on my way home with Micah right behind me."

His sigh was barely audible, but the sense of relief she heard warmed her heart. She knew he cared for her, but she realized that he had trouble showing it. Usually, like tonight, he cast orders around, telling her and anyone in the vicinity of her what to do. It was his way of showing concern.

"You could have come yourself."

"No. You said you needed time."

Yeah, and that had been stupid. "It didn't mean you couldn't come by."

"It does if you aren't going to let me touch you."

"We don't have sex every time we see each other."

"If I touch you, there is no doubt. We will." Each word was bit out. The irritation in his voice made her smile. Had she thought this man cold? Jesus, he was anything but. A cold, hard exterior, yes, but there was something gooey beneath.

"I wouldn't mind that."

Her quiet words were met with silence. "Are you sure?"

She didn't hesitate. "Yes."

Lights flashed in her mirror and she realized an SUV was next to Micah. He sped up, apparently not wanting to let the vehicle between them. She glanced away to look in front of her, then she heard the sound of metal against metal. She looked up in her mirror again and saw the SUV shove Micah's vette to the curb. She watched in horror as the vette flew over it and into a wall, the front end of his vehicle collapsing under the force of the impact.

"Oh my God!"

"What?" Evan yelled.

"An SUV just forced Micah off the road."

"What is it doing now?"

The SUV was speeding toward her back bumper, intent on going after her.

"Fuck."

"May, I'm on my way. Where are you?"

"I just passed Kahala Mall."

"Sit tight."

She could say nothing as she watched the SUV come up beside her. Before she could hit her brakes, it swerved, into her side. She finally slammed on her brakes, but it was too late, she was spinning out of control. The dizzying rays of light flashed before her eyes and her stomach threatened revolt. She dropped the phone, Evan's voice yelling at her as it turned off.

She hit the curb and slammed into the guardrail. Thankfully, they had not been on a long stretch of highway with no shoulder and just cliffs and water below. Her head hit the airbag as it deployed. Her head was fuzzy, she couldn't seem to gather her thoughts. The need to get away, to escape had her turning the ignition. Of course, it didn't start with the air bag deployed. Someone tapped the window and she whipped around to find herself staring down the barrel of a gun.

Evan raced through the streets, cursing himself for not being there. He had thought Micah would be enough to keep someone from her, that once they saw his friend, whoever it was would go on their merry way as they had for weeks. But he had been wrong...horribly wrong.

The terror he heard in her voice still rang in his ears. He tried calling a couple of times, but it had rang and rang,

He called 911 as he broke laws to get to her. He just hoped his major fuck-up didn't cost him the one thing he needed to survive.

May opened the door and Lee wrapped her hand around her upper arm and pulled her from the car. Sharp bright pain radiated from her lower arm and she found herself unable to move it.

"You have been a real pain in the ass, you know?"

May stumbled forward. "I have no idea what you're talking about."

Lee looked around, apparently trying to see if anyone was watching them. Unless Evan called someone closer, there would be no one for a few moments.

The smaller woman slammed May against the car, releasing her arm. Damn, she was little but apparently had hands of steel.

"You fired me from a job, bitch."

"You were stealing."

Lee shrugged. "I did it at other jobs."

"So we should just let you get away with it? This is what all of the letters, the pictures, the pain you caused me is about? Some fucking job? Your father has more money than God. You don't even have to work."

"You fired me. Worse, you kept me from getting involved with the boss."

Her brain was still scrambled from the wreck. Was Lee actually saying she stalked her for weeks because she fired her? From a waitressing job? "Jesus. I can't believe you're standing here threatening to kill me because I fired you and Chris wanted nothing to do with your skanky ass."

"Shut the fuck up."

The gun wavered slightly and Lee looked around again.

"You must have one sad, pathetic life if you have turned to

stalking someone who fired you."

"He moaned your name!"

May's brain apparently didn't function in the way crazy ass stalker's brains did because this conversation was making little sense.

"Chris moaned my name?"

Lee's eyes narrowed. "Evan. The last time we were having sex, he moaned your name then he fucking dumped me. You'd fired me, kept me from hooking up with the boss, then my lover, *my* lover, said your name as he came."

For a moment, she let that knowledge sink in, warm her. Even before they'd slept together he had wanted her. He had said that, but she hadn't been so sure about it. May couldn't stop the smile that curved her lips.

"You were always such a goody-two-shoes bitch. You could never give him what he needed, not like I could. He needs someone like me."

"Evan doesn't want you."

"Shut up!" The gun wavered again and Lee's breathing became more erratic. "It wasn't until I had him, until I knew he was like me, that I knew Evan was for me."

"Apparently not, because he's been with me for the last month."

"Shut up!"

May knew that angering Lee would be the only chance she had. If she lost control, May might be able to overcome the crazy bitch. Micah hadn't made it out of the mangled car. It was really deserted at the moment, so she didn't think she would have help until Evan arrived. If he'd been at his house, he was still at least five minutes away.

May knew she needed to distract her. Lee had a bad temper

and usually acted without thinking. There was a good chance she would attack physically, not with the gun. "He didn't stay around with you. He came to me, became my lover. In fact, we've lasted longer than you two did." May shook her head. "And he doesn't call out your name when we're making love."

The statement had the effect May wanted. Lee flew toward her with a scream. Apparently forgetting that she had a gun, she knocked May to the ground. Anger welled up. The pain and worry this woman had caused her, her family, her friends, Evan over such petty things. All of them had worried, agonized over the letters, the things being done to her. All because this woman and her fucking pride. May used that anger and a good dose of fear and shoved the palm of her hand against Lee's nose. She heard the crack of bone, then felt warm liquid wet her hand.

"You bitch! You broke my nose."

May used the distraction to shove at the smaller woman and try and pin her to the ground. But anger was nothing against crazy rage. Lee slammed the gun against May's temple with such force her world spun, and she felt a warm trickle of blood dripping down her face. Lee used her momentary lapse to force herself up and over May.

Lee punched May in the face, the full force of it threatening May's stomach. Another hit, another smack, and May felt the world spin and then start to fall away. The screech of tires barely reached her, but the sounds of sirens screamed through her senses as Lee battered at her. Then, mercifully it stopped, and her weight was lifted away from May's chest. The scream was filled with rage and fear.

"Leave me alone, you asshole," Lee screeched.

"We'll take it from here, Chambers."

May tried to open her eyes, but they were too heavy.

217

"May?"

Even over the sirens and Lee's screaming, May heard him. She used all her strength to open her eyes. Red and blue lights flashed and people were tossing orders around.

"Evan." She whimpered because her own voice sounded like a bullhorn in her head.

He kneeled beside her. "Shhh, baby, just rest. The ambulance is on the way."

"Micah..."

"There are people with him."

"Sir, you have to move."

Evan brushed a lock of hair away from her face. "I'll be here. Your father and brother are on the way. But I'll be there at the hospital."

"Sir, move it, or I'll get one of the officers to help you move."

He did as ordered, then a woman's face came into view. "Ms. Aiona? Can you hear me?"

"Yes."

"Do you know if you have anything broken?"

"Not sure. I broke her nose."

The woman chuckled. "Good girl. Now we're going to get you on a gurney and get you to the hospital."

Everything seemed to be dimming, the lights and sounds. Black crowded her vision.

"Ms. Aiona!"

"May!"

She couldn't fight the pain anymore and felt herself drift away.

Chapter Nineteen

Evan paced the emergency room, his anger and fear still churning his stomach. They had been here for an hour. It felt like days. If anything happened to her, he didn't know what he would do.

"Take a seat, Evan."

He looked over at May's father who sat patiently waiting to be called back to see his daughter. His calm behavior grated on Evan's raw nerves.

"I can't. If I had been just a minute later..."

"But you weren't. You made it there in time. And the doctors seem to think the worst thing she has is a concussion."

Evan shook his head. "You say that like it's no big deal."

"I've been through worse."

"Really? How is that? What would be worse than losing your daughter?"

May's brother broke in. "I'm going to get us some coffee. I have a feeling we might need it."

Once Kai left, Daniel looked at Evan, his face appearing older than Evan had ever seen it. Now he looked all of his fifty-five years.

"I've been here, you know? Thirteen years ago, I stood where you are, trying to tell myself if I had done something, if I had been driving her home from work, she'd be alive."

Evan knew he spoke of Kayla, his wife.

"I never thought..."

"I understand your feelings. You love her, I can see it in your reaction, but I knew the first time I saw you together. You look at her the same way I'm sure I looked at Kayla. She was my lifeline in the world, the one person who could make everything right. Losing her ripped me apart."

"How did you handle it?" Evan asked.

"Day by day." He smiled at Evan's snort. "Trite but true. The worst thing is knowing there was nothing I could have done. If it had been me at the wheel, we would have both been gone, leaving the kids alone. Oh, they would have had their grandfather, but they needed me. There are too many things we can't control. What if I had driven home? What if the driver who'd been picked up three times in two months for drunk driving had his license taken away or had been in jail? Life is full of what ifs. If you worry about them—and what you can't do to change them—your life will mean nothing."

"It's because of me that she went through this."

Her father shook his head. "You terrorized her, defiled her car, ran her off the road and pistol whipped her?"

Evan tossed him a nasty look. "You know what I mean."

"We have no idea what was going on in that woman's mind. But I will smack you upside the head if you use this to pull away from May."

Before he could answer Daniel, the doctor came in. "Mr. Aiona, May is awake. I thought you and your son would like to see her."

"She'll want to see Evan."

The doctor glanced at him. "Husband?"

Evan shook his head.

"I'm sorry, but she's in ICU right now. I can't let anyone but family in there."

"But he's family...or will be."

Evan shot May's father a surprised look who winked at him.

"Oh, a fiancé?" The doctor studied him and then said, "I think I might be able to bend the rules."

Kai caught them before they got to the ICU doors. He gave them all their coffees. The doctor frowned at Kai because of the two person limit, but he let it go.

"Now I want you all to understand that she looks worse than it really is. The swelling is bad, but that happens with things like this. The bruising is worse, but thankfully she has no broken bones in her face. Her arm is broken, but that is easier to heal than facial fractures."

Even with the doctor's warning, Evan was not prepared for the sight of her bruised appearance. Her eyes were so swollen, Evan had doubts she would be able to open them any time soon. An explosion of purple and yellow bruises marred her skin and her face was misshapen.

"Lord." Her father's whispered comment sounded like a prayer. Evan had lost his faith years before, but he would pray to anyone to save her from the pain he knew she would feel when she woke up.

"The swelling should go down in the next twelve hours. Her concussion isn't severe and she was able to talk to us coherently. That's a very good sign."

He shot the doctor a look. They didn't say things like that unless there was a chance of complications.

"But?"

"It's a head injury. While she should be fine, I can't give her a one hundred percent."

Evan curled his fingers into the palms of his hands, wanting to strangle the bastard. This was his damn job to save people. If anything...

"You better calm yourself down for when she does wake up. I'm not a miracle worker, and there is always a chance of complications with head injuries. But she is very strong, and all the tests we've done look good."

Evan ordered himself to calm down. Attacking the doctor would be useless, stupid and misguided. His need to hit something, to beat it to a bloody pulp had nothing to do with those around him, but rather with his own failure.

"I'll leave you alone." The doctor turned to leave the three of them, but looked over his shoulder at him. "She kept telling me she broke the other woman's nose. She's a fighter."

Silence enveloped the three men and the woman they all loved. Evan stood at the foot of the bed and watched her brother and father hold her hands.

"She always was a fighter," Kai said, amusement lacing his words. "I was bigger, stronger, and I swear she wouldn't give up when we were kids. When I got much too big for her to handle, she started using that quick mind to fight me. I never stood a chance."

Her father moved away from the bed and motioned toward Evan.

"Come. You sit here and hold her hand. She'll want to see you when she wakes up."

Evan hesitated, then moved and took the seat on her right side.

"I'm going to call my father and Danny. They don't like you

using the cell in ICU."

The door closed behind him, and Evan waited for the recriminations to come. Kai wasn't as kind and understanding as his father.

"She loves you, you know?"

Evan nodded.

"You don't have to tell me how you feel. It's written on your face."

He said nothing and Kai continued.

"She's had a thing for you for awhile. I thought it was a crush, but apparently not."

Evan stroked a strand of her hair. "No."

"I'll tell you this because I love her. Even as much as I like you, and the rest of my family likes you, I'll rip you apart if you hurt her."

"Too late."

Kai rolled his eyes. "Lord, are you always this dramatic?"

"I'm not good enough for her."

"I know."

Evan looked at him. "I'm the son of a crackwhore."

Kai shrugged. "Who apparently didn't follow her into the family business."

Evan felt a bubble of laughter threaten to escape. He cleared his throat. "No. But there are things about me, things that make me unworthy of her."

"Spare me, Chambers. You want to go all dramatic and blame your fear on your background, be my guest. But if you are just going to hurt her, leave now. She doesn't need a man who is too much of a coward to love her."

Anger came first, boiling in his blood, and had him

dropping May's hand with the idea of wrapping his around her brother's neck.

Then he saw Kai's face, the amusement. He didn't look a bit scared.

"Men have been hurt for saying things that weren't as bad."

Kai's smile widened. "You don't scare me, Chambers. I work in and around the docks. I know how to handle myself. Besides, you wouldn't hurt me because that would hurt May. And since you're whipped, you won't do it."

Evan stared at him for a second then chuckled. "Jesus, you're an ass."

"But one that she loves."

"If both of you don't shut the hell up, I'm going to have the doctor throw you out," May croaked out.

"May," Kai yelled.

"Jesus, Kai. You trying to split my head in two?"

"I have to go get Dad."

He leaned in to kiss her forehead. Then left them alone.

She turned her head to Evan. "I bet I look like crap."

"You've had better days."

She chuckled and then drew in a quick, pain-filled breath.

He squeezed her hand. "You need to rest."

"Micah?"

"Broken leg, concussion. Well enough to bitch about going home, but they want to keep him overnight."

"I…"

He could see she was struggling, so he shook his head. "Rest. Your family's going to be here any minute so you need to save your strength."

She nodded and her eyes shut. The doctor came in,

followed by her father and brother. Evan stood.

"No, you stay," Daniel insisted.

Evan shook his head. "I need to check on Micah and get his care set up. He's going to need some help the first few days. Plus, I need to put a call into the club and my own work. With all of this, we'll need someone to take over in both places."

Daniel nodded. "You make sure you get back here, ASAP."

"Or?"

"I'll come after you with my gun."

For the first time since getting May's call, Evan laughed. "No problem, bruddah. It's going to take an armored tank to get me away from her from now on."

"I'm bored."

Danny ignored her and continued reading his sports magazine. Butthead. He'd been ignoring her since her last griping session. Calling him a snot-nosed know-it- all probably was the wrong thing to say. And she wanted to apologize. But every time she opened her mouth, something horrible came out. It was like she wasn't in control of anything. It had been three days and she was ready to go home, but the doctor would not hear of it until today. She was bored, ready to get out of the hospital with the antiseptic smells and the damned people waking her up in the middle of the night to check her vitals.

"Did you hear me?"

He nodded.

"And?"

He shrugged.

She wanted to growl, but instead she lapsed into silence. Truthfully, she should be nicer to Danny as he was the last man standing. Every freaking male in her life, including Chris, had gone running to the hills. Not one of them had the nerve to put up with her bitching. Danny was oblivious to it. He let everything roll off his back. That just pissed her off even more.

She opened her mouth to apologize to him, and the door opened. Evan came in pushing a wheelchair. One of the staff followed him, meekly casting glances in her direction. Jesus, she even scared the admin staff here. The woman looked ready to run at the first word.

"Guess what, May? The doctor has released you."

A nurse came in with a mutinous look lighting her eyes. Oh, God, she's the one May had called a battleax when she ordered May to bed that first day.

Without much problem, the nurse removed her IV. The clerk had her all signed out and ready to go. Less than ten minutes later, Evan was wheeling her into the elevator.

"I don't know what you did, but thank you."

"Did?"

"To bust me out of here. Doctor Franks refused to let me go. He said something about my concussion, blah, blah."

He backed her onto the elevator and Danny hit the button for the first floor.

"You got that wrong. I think the staff all signed a petition to get rid of you. Dr. Franks was facing a mutiny if he didn't get rid of you."

Danny hooted with laughter as she gave Evan a dirty look.

"He has your number, Maylea. Lord, you are the worst patient."

"Just for that, I'm not going to apologize for what I called you earlier."

He shrugged. "I am a know-it-all. Of course, that is because I do know it all."

226

Evan chuckled. "Better than what she called that nurse in there, not to mention Chris."

"He was a coward."

"Any man who isn't scared when a woman starts crying is an idiot."

Her face burned with embarrassment when she remembered Chris backing out of the room saying he couldn't handle another crying woman, especially one calling him names. She was probably going to get fired just for that.

Neither Danny nor Evan said anything as they walked through the lobby. Evan put the brake on her chair, squatted in front of her and smiled. Her heart did that little happy dance it did every time he smiled, but she silently pushed it aside.

"Now. I am going to get my truck. Danny is going to stand guard and make sure you don't scare any more of the staff, not to mention visitors and other patients."

"I wasn't that bad."

"Honey, you were worse." He kissed her nose and then ambled away in direction of the parking garage.

"What does he mean he's getting his truck?"

Danny shrugged. "I think it would be better to go in the truck, right? With my little car, you're going to feel every little bump."

Nodding, she closed her eyes, enjoying the sun warming her face. It slipped over her skin, heating her. She could taste the salt in the air, enjoyed the noise of the passing traffic. God, she needed this. Being stuck in the hospital had felt like prison.

"Here he is."

She opened her eyes and saw Evan ease his truck into the passenger pickup zone. Danny bent down and kissed her cheek. "I'll see you later."

She opened her mouth to ask where he was going, but Danny was already walking away.

Bracing her weight on her one good hand, she tried to stand. She'd already been walking on a regular basis, but all the sudden she seemed exhausted. It was as if she'd run a 3K.

Evan came hurrying up to her. "What the hell are you doing?"

"Standing."

"Damned fool woman."

"Whatarrrgh—"

He bent down and scooped her up out of the chair. "You don't have the sense God gave a gnat."

With a gentleness that eased some of her irritation, he slid her onto the front seat and buckled her seatbelt. She could see him muttering as he walked around the hood of the car.

"Rest."

She wanted to argue with him, but she was exhausted and so did as he ordered.

Chapter Twenty

Evan put the truck in park and then turned it off. He glanced at May and was happy to see that she was still asleep. He knew she hadn't been comfortable in the hospital. She had needed control and she had lost it, thanks to Lee. God, that fucking bitch was lucky she was in jail. If not, he would hunt her down and make her pay for what she'd done to May. Evan had never wanted to make a woman hurt until three days ago.

And she was crazy, loony. There was a good chance the insanity plea might work. According to Officer Carino, she just kept rambling about everything May had taken from her. Apparently the woman blamed May for every wrong she'd had done to her. From being arrested for shoplifting to the day she was fired from Dupree's, the woman was convinced that May had a hand in it all.

He sighed and pulled his temper back under control. It wouldn't get him anywhere, and May didn't need it. Her bruises had faded, but there was still enough evidence to tell anyone who saw her she'd been through hell.

As quietly as possible, he slipped out of the truck and went to unlock the front door to the house. When he returned to the truck, he opened the door and picked her up off the seat. She stirred and wrapped her one good arm around his neck, snuggling her head on his shoulder, her mouth against the base of his neck.

"Evan?" She slowly came awake as he carried her into his house. He had pulled a lot of strings, not to mention bullied her doctor, to get her out. He needed her here, in his house, by his side. It was as simple as that. Now that she was out of the woods, there was no need for her to be in the hospital. He could take better care for her.

"What are we doing here?"

He stepped over the threshold, May in his arms and paused. The reality of what he'd just done made him smile. He shut the door with his foot.

"I'm going to take care of you."

She raised her head so swiftly she knocked his chin.

"Ow."

"Well, you should watch what you're doing," he said.

He set her down on his couch and then rubbed his chin. "Damn. And people tell me I have a hard head."

She moved to stand but Evan shook his head.

"You can fight me all you want, but I'm going to take care of you."

"I'll just call my father."

He sat down on his coffee table and offered her a grin, thinking of the conversation he'd had with Daniel that morning.

"I wouldn't bet on it."

Her eyes narrowed and he watched her temper move over her face. "Why not?"

"Your father and I came to an understanding."

"What the hell does that mean?"

He shook his head. "First, I'd like to tell you a story."

She had opened her mouth "What?"

"Promise me you'll be patient. It's about my childhood."

She instantly stilled, her gaze glued to his. He took her hand in his and swallowed the fear that threatened to choke him.

"I guess you know that I had a less than stellar upbringing."

She nodded.

"It was probably worse than anything you could think of. My mother was a crackwhore."

"That doesn't matter to me."

He brought her hand to his lips. "Thanks. Now shut up." Her mulish expression made him laugh. "I'm not sure I would've ever figured you for a sub if you hadn't signed that contract with Micah.

Her expression softened and she opened her mouth to respond. He shook his head. "Let me get this out. My father spent some time in prison, then disappeared, so it was just me and Mom for as long as I remember. Anyway, it couldn't have been easy raising a son when she was so young, just seventeen, high school dropout with a young kid to take care of."

She opened her mouth, but he placed his fingers against her lips. "Let me finish."

Understanding filled those Caribbean eyes and his heart squeezed. Just a little thing, but he felt it all the way down to his soul.

"Mom always had a thing for drugs, but when crack got a hold of her...she seemed to lose all sense of reality. It wasn't long before she was bringing men back to the apartment to service."

Her eyes widened but she said nothing.

"Yeah. When I say crackwhore, I mean it in every sense.

Smack was her favorite and that isn't cheap. Soon, she couldn't keep up with the demand her own body wanted. So, she figured out a way to make even more money. There were always men who had a taste for young boys."

"Oh, Evan."

He studied her face. He had expected pity or horror, not the sympathy and love he saw in her eyes. There was another squeeze to his heart.

"I could lie and say it wasn't bad. But it was bad, especially since she didn't care if they got a little rough. It was no skin off her nose if they left me a little bruised. Sometimes they paid extra for that."

"That fucking bitch."

He laughed, he couldn't help it. It was just what he would expect her to say. She was probably already trying to formulate a way to find his mother.

He shook his head. "Forget it, she's dead."

"What?"

"I know you. You were trying to figure out just where to find her, what resources you had. She's dead. One night a john beat the living hell out of her. I found her the next morning. I'd disappeared the night before, hid out around the area trying to avoid anyone she might bring home that night."

"That must have been horrible to find your mother that way."

He shook his head again. "You want to know the truth? I was relieved. Someone had done what I had wanted to do for years. I called the cops and ended up in the system. At that moment, I promised myself I wouldn't have kids."

"Why?"

He pulled in a deep breath and released it. "I was convinced that with her blood running through me, I was tainted. I couldn't be sure I wouldn't hurt my own children."

"How old where you?"

"Ten."

"But I've never seen anything mean in you, not that way. You go out of your way to be nice. I cannot even imagine what it must have been like. You are a good man, despite your childhood. Many people would use that as an excuse to not try hard. You accomplished so much with your life. You should be proud."

Her compliments were balm to his battered soul. But there were things he had to tell her, one in particular. "I did things to ensure I could never have a woman like you. I dated women like Lee. I also engaged in ménages." He saw the way her eyes lit up. "Forget it. There ain't no way another man is touching you."

She pouted. "Spoilsport."

"One of those ménages involved Chris and Cynthia."

She didn't say anything for a moment. "But you aren't involved anymore."

"I wasn't really involved, it was all about them. A onetime deal."

"Oh, when she gave up control. I wondered how that happened, what they did. But she knows how squeamish I am about hearing sexual things about Chris. It's like hearing about my brothers having sex. Ick."

"I think you're missing the point."

"You had a ménage with Chris and Cynthia, I get it. We both have a sexual past. Granted, mine is kind of boring compared to yours, but there you have it."

"I had sex with your friend."

She thought for a second and then shrugged. "Knowing

you, you've probably slept with more than one person I know. It wasn't while we were together. That would be different. That would involve knives and certain appendages that you value highly. Oh, and telling my brother. You know he works at the docks...he can make you disappear."

For a second, he couldn't respond. "You continue to amaze me."

Her smile widened. "That's me, amazing May. So go on."

He wanted to pull her against him, kiss her, tell her how much he loved her. But if he did, he never would get all of the story out.

"See, my father had been busted for rape and assault, and my mother was a dead crackwhore who sold her son for drugs. I thought the best thing to have happen was for the family bloodline to die."

She pursed her lips in thought. "What makes you so sure you can even father children?"

He laughed. "Jesus, May, only you would insult me when trying to lift me up."

"You say you avoided getting serious because of the chance of children. You might be sterile."

"God, you are a pill, you know that."

Her smile faded. "That is what you were dreaming about that night? About your mother...and those men."

He nodded, never taken his gaze from hers. "I had thought we could be involved and nothing would change. My conscience was trying to tell me something, I think."

"What?"

"I love you, May."

Tears filled her eyes as she patted his hand. "No, you don't but that's nice."

It took him a moment to understand just what she had said. "I do love you."

"You feel obligated because of what happened, but you don't really love me."

He stared at her for a second. "Listen, woman, I swear to the Lord above I love you. If you don't believe that, well, too damn bad."

"I love you. You know that. But you don't need to feel as if you have to lie. I will still love you. I had already decided to call you that night."

Some of the tightness in his chest loosened. "Yeah?"

"Yeah. So there's no reason to lie."

"You know, it figures that you would do this to me. Never before have I told another person I loved them. I finally do it, and you don't believe me. I spent a whole fucking day shopping for a ring, and you go on and on about how I don't love you."

"A ring?"

"Yeah. Fat lot of good it did me to come prepared. I finally find a woman who's my whole life and she's too stupid to realize it. Even after I tell her how I love her, she doesn't believe me."

He stood up and started pacing the room and May watched him. Some of what he was saying was sinking in. Did he really buy her a ring, as in marriage? Her head was still whirling with what he had revealed and she couldn't seem to catch up.

"Go back to the ring thing."

He snarled at her over his shoulder and she had to bite her bottom lip to keep from smiling. Warm joy bounced through her, filling her heart as she continued to watch him pace around the room.

"You know, this is what's wrong with women. You do what

235

they want, then they gripe at you. Damned if you can ever please one."

"Evan."

"What?"

"Ask me."

He stopped and looked at her. The anger faded from his eyes and tears filled hers as she saw the love she felt reflected back. He moved to her then, kneeling beside the couch. He reached into his shirt pocket and pulled out a box. He opened it and within the satin lining sat a solitaire square-cut diamond.

"I love you, May. You're the only woman for me, the only lover I need for the rest of my life. Marry me."

Elation exploded through her and she smiled at him as she felt tears slip down her cheeks.

"Yes. I'll marry you."

He slipped the ring on her finger and then leaned in for a kiss. A touch of mouth, tongue, and then he was gone. She frowned and tried to follow him.

"No, you aren't up to it. There'll be time for that later."

She wanted to argue, but she knew he was right. Even right now, she was tired and in need of a nap. He picked her up off the couch, sat down in her spot and settled her on his lap. His heart thumped against her temple and his body heat surrounded her.

"I have some champagne, but figure you can't have any. We can save it for the engagement party."

She nodded and snuggled against his chest, happy in the warmth of his love, and drifted off into blissful dreams.

About the Author

Born to an Air Force family at an Army hospital, Melissa has always been a little bit screwy. She was further warped by her years of watching Monty Python and her strange family. Her love of romance novels developed after accidentally picking up a Linda Howard book. Since her first release in 2004, Melissa has had close to 30 short stories, novellas and novels released with seven different publishers in a variety of genres and time periods. Those releases included an Eppie nomination and two CAPA nominations, along with a multitude of best sellers and recommended reads. Her contemporary, A Little Harmless Sex became an international best seller in June of 2005.

Since she was a military brat, she vowed never to marry military. Alas, Fate always has her way with mortals. Her husband is an Air Force major, and together they have their own military brats, two girls, an adopted dog daughter and they live wherever the military sticks them. Which until recently always involved heat and bugs only seen on the Animal Discovery Channel. In her spare time, she reads, complains about bugs, travels, cooks, reads some more, and tries to convince her family that she truly is a delicate genius. She has yet to achieve her last goal.

If you want to know more about Melissa, stop by the following websites:

www.melissaschroeder.net,

twitter.com/melschroeder,

http://www.facebook.com/pages/Melissa-Schroeder/17997114885.

She loves to hear from her readers so be sure to drop Melissa a note:

Melissa@melissaschroeder.net

or

Melissa Schroeder

PO Box 2706

Manassas, VA 20108

Is it love or just a little harmless pleasure?

A Little Harmless Pleasure
© *2008 Melissa Schroeder*

Cynthia Myers meets Chris Dupree at her former fiancé's wedding. After a little dancing, and champagne, she ends up back in Chris's hotel room. For one night of down and dirty sex. That's it, that's all. He lives far away, and she has other things to do...like get a life.

Chris is a switch. He likes to dominate but he also likes to play the role of a submissive from time to time. His last relationship with a sub turned nasty and since then, he has shied away from anything but straight vanilla sex. When he meets Cynthia, he finds a woman who could change his mind. His mate. The only problem is he has to convince her.

In a carefully orchestrated seduction, Chris teaches Cynthia about submission and dominance, allowing her take the reins. As he leads her through pleasures she thought she'd never experience, Cynthia's self confidence soars and she finds herself falling in love with him. But, when he asks for submission in the bedroom, can she surrender to prove her love or was it all about a little harmless pleasure?

Warning, this book contains: Lots of sex, of course; bondage and submission done in a tasteful but wonderfully arousing way, propositions from a drunken woman, hot phone sex, southern accents, Hawaiian scenery, and OH MY, a m/f/m ménage that will send tingles all the way to your toes, along with other various body parts. A glass of ice cold water for refreshment is recommended while reading.

Available now in ebook and print from Samhain Publishing.

CPSIA information can be obtained at www.ICGtesting.com
Printed in the USA
267147BV00002B/1/P